PEOPLE IN TROUBLE

PEOPLE IN TROUBLE

SARAH SCHULMAN

E. P. DUTTON   NEW YORK

Published in the United States by E. P. Dutton, a division of Penguin Books USA Inc., 2 Park Avenue, New York, N.Y. 10016.

Published simultaneously in Canada by Fitzhenry and Whiteside, Limited, Toronto.

Library of Congress Cataloging-in-Publication Data

Schulman, Sarah, 1958–
People in trouble / Sarah Schulman.
p.   cm.
ISBN: 0-525-24835-8
I. Title.
PS3569.C5393P46   1990
813'.54—dc20   89-17130
                                                                CIP

Designed by Margo D. Barooshian

10 9 8 7 6 5 4 3 2 1

First Edition

This book is dedicated with great love
to Maxine Wolfe

ACKNOWLEDGMENTS

△△△

Different friends read this book in various versions. Each had a wholly unique and personal set of criteria that they brought to the project. I thank them for their time and attention, especially Maxine Wolfe, Bettina Berch, Abigail Child, Christie Cassidy, Meg Wolitzer, Julia Scher, David Leavitt, Shelley Wald, Michael Korie, Stewart Wallace, Beryl Satter, Robert Hilferty and Ana Maria Simo.

People in Trouble was financed, in part, through generous grants and loans from Charlie Schulman, Susan Seizer, my parents, Jennifer Miller, Abigail Child, Rachel Pfeffer, Beryl Satter, Diane Cleaver with Sanford Greenburger Associates, the Mac-Dowell Colony, Cummington Community for the Arts, and the Money for Women/Barbara Deming Memorial Fund. I thank them for their support and patience.

My editor, Carole DeSanti, engaged this book with a high level of concentration and creativity. I am grateful for her insightful and intelligent contributions throughout the many drafts.

It is not the consciousness of men that determines their being, but their social being that determines their consciousness.

—KARL MARX

PEOPLE IN TROUBLE

KATE

△△

It was the beginning of the end of the world but not everyone noticed right away. Some people were dying. Some people were busy. Some people were cleaning their houses while the war movie played on television.

The cigarette in the mouth of the woman behind the register was cemented with purple lipstick. She had lipstick smeared on her smock. Tiny caterpillars of gray ash decorated the sticky glass countertop.

"I'll take these two," Kate told her, holding each bra in a different hand.

"You'd better try them on," the clerk answered with a quick professional assessment. "These are too big for you, miss, and after a certain age you can't count on growing any more in that direction."

"They're not for me," Kate said, enjoying herself thoroughly. "Cash please."

Which one would Molly wear first? She held them in her hands absentmindedly running the material through her fingers. Kate would see them on Molly's body before she touched them in place. There was the demure lace that opened from the front, like walking in through a garden gate. Then there was the really dirty push-up that didn't need to open. Kate could lift Molly's breasts right out over the top. Kate held them in her hands. She could run her fingers over the lace and feel its texture as she felt Molly's nipples changing underneath.

"Leopard-print crotchless panties on sale," the woman added, folding ashes into the wrapping paper. "Maybe your friend would like a pair of these too. Great with skirts."

It would be three days before she saw Molly again. Kate climbed the stairs to her lover's apartment and left the package by the front door with a private note.

When they did meet on schedule, Kate felt a certain nervous eroticism wondering which one Molly had chosen, which one was waiting for her under Molly's soft blouse.

"You're sexy," Kate told her at dusk. "You have languid eyes and beautiful breasts. I gift wrap them as a present to myself. Your breasts are beautiful, creamy and sweet."

She pressed her hands from Molly's face to her chest and felt the shape of the lace underneath, but then kept going back to that wisp waist and the sloping shelf at the end of her back.

"But it's your ass that turns me on tonight. Tonight it's your ass that's hot."

Then she thought *Am I really saying these things?*

Molly pulled her out of the early streetlight and into a shadow, so the gypsy reading fortunes in the storefront across the way wouldn't have to push her kids into the back room out of sight. Molly arched her ass, sliding over Kate's flesh so that Kate felt her lover's warm body against her chest and the cool brick wall on her back.

"Let's go up on your roof," Kate said.

"You really want to do it, don't you?" Molly laughed, her neck smelling like cucumber.

"Guess so."

"Let's go," Molly said, looking sparkly and quite lovely. "Besides, there's not that much time left."

There was a change, then, to a quiet happiness and a certain sense of contentment that accompanied them up the stairs. On top of the building there was only heaven and a radio rising from illuminated shapes. A man was smoking somewhere—they could hear him cough. The radio was a thin reed. There was a child to the right and silverware clattering, all below. There were undiscernible cars, frequently, and a chime and a voice.

ΔΔΔΔΔΔΔΔΔΔΔΔΔΔΔΔΔΔΔΔΔΔΔΔΔΔΔΔΔΔΔΔΔΔΔΔΔΔΔΔΔΔΔΔΔΔΔΔΔΔΔΔΔΔΔΔΔΔΔΔΔΔΔΔΔΔΔΔΔΔΔ

There was a fight in the coffee shop that morning that got out of hand very quickly. Then Peter walked an entire block to avoid some kind of turf war between two young black men who were probably selling crack.

We New Yorkers always have something else to fear, he told himself, turning up University Place. *First it was herpes, this year it's crossfire.*

Originally he'd just been wandering, but was seduced, on the spot, by the idea of a bowling alley occupying two floors of an office building, and decided to duck in.

Where he grew up, bowling alleys had always been white stucco boxes with a giant-size pin towering over the parking lot. The bowlers had been divided into two groups; league competitors and amateurs on dates. Anyone could pick out the regulars because they looked so serious. The women had that lacquered hair, teased and dyed red, bleached or frosted. They wore over-size bowling jackets with their husbands' names embroidered on their backs. The men had regulation jackets that fit, regulation shoes and little personalized carrying cases for their bowling balls.

City people, on the other hand, didn't take tenpins to heart. They had a thousand other fascinating ways to occupy their time and so retreated, one rainy Sunday a year, to broken shoes and chipped balls. In Manhattan, bowling is symbolic. It is nostalgia for a simpler life.

Peter stepped into an elevator that was two by three with a skinny Chinese operator chain-smoking Kents. There was no ventilation, so passengers held their breath until the old contraption clanked to the second floor. There, the hand-operated iron-grate door creaked open to reveal a faded hall of crashing pins and a few timeless Italian kids yelling "Joey." Most everyone else, though, seemed too modern to be bowling. It wasn't a sport to them, it was only a kick.

When Peter was growing up in New Hampshire, the light had been delicate, not globbed on like wet plaster New York style. Night in Manhattan is never dark, only the days can be. But New England nights were black underneath, covered with a layer of starlight and then midnight blue. That elusive color showed itself only twice a year; once during the rainy period of early April that felt like fall and then in the clarity days of October that smelled like spring. It was a symbol of sensual confusion.

As a child he'd ride on his bike or be in a car at night and every so often he'd pass a house in which there was a yellow glow for someone to come home to. He would sit in it later, wearing pajamas, waiting for two headlights, more pale yellow than the kitchen's straw. They threw shadows on the driveway that were followed by the crunch of gravel.

That was how he remembered his mother most clearly. She would step out of the car in her pink uniform and white shoes, kicking them off first thing. Then she'd count the tips. Every night until he went to work himself Peter watched his mother divide up all the change, starting with the pennies, saving the quarters for last. She'd lean back in her chair so they could stare at the coins together. She knew exactly what the stacks could and could not do for her.

After Peter was put to bed, his mother spoke briefly to herself. She'd talk back to a customer, list everything that had gone un-done, recall or invent conversation. Then she'd pour a whiskey. He could hear the ice clinking in the kitchen. She'd turn on the radio a shade too low and that was the last sound in his head when Peter fell asleep at night; the murmur of the radio with his mother's occasional duet.

The particular yellow that brought her home from work was the first chapter in his lifetime of light and stayed strong as a memory until he'd finally applied it thirty years later to a small musical uptown. In the third act the hero, having escaped over a prison wall, burst into song. After the last note of the final refrain, the police switched on their ignition, trapping him in the eye of their headlights. It pleased Peter every night to see the convict's expression of fright, hearing the audience gasp, when he knew all along that it was only his mother driving home from work with an apronful of nickels.

Memory, he thought, *is part of what light means to me.*

The rented bowling shoes matched the pins; white, with red stripes. They smelled of leather and foot sweat and disinfectant spray. They were too big. Peter walked through the place picking up balls as he went along, trying them out. He needed one that was heavy enough, one that had grip.

In the next lane was a teenage girl in tight brown curls who was also bowling alone. He saw her sleepy brown eyes and the moles on her face. She dressed the way girls do who don't realize how beautiful they are because they don't have enough experi-ence in the world to compare. She wore everything so tight he wanted to touch her all over. The name on her scorecard said Shelley. Peter watched her approach. She always turned her wrist at the last minute and each bowl went directly into the gutter.

"Keep your wrists straight," he said. "And you'll hit the pins."

"I don't really care about that," she said. "I'm just wasting time."

∆∆

She had a purse, like girls do, and sticking out of it was a book Peter would not have associated with a girl like that.

He bowled a strike.

"You're reading O'Neill," he said.

"It's for school," she said. "I'm not really reading it. I'm just carrying it around."

"My first design was a college production of *Mourning Becomes Electra*," he said, thumbing through the pages. "Here, see." He pointed to a particular spot on the paper and placed it in front of her. "O'Neill, sitting comfortably on a Provincetown beach decided that the piece should be played in a *luminous mist*. That's a hell of an introduction to basic design."

"I'm going to the bathroom," she said.

Shelley came back with a new pack of Marlboros. She hit it against her palm so the tobacco would tighten up and burn more evenly. Then she pulled off the cellophane wrapper.

"Do you know what's written on a Marlboro box?" he asked.

" 'Cigarette smoking can be hazardous to your health'?"

"Besides that."

"No."

He took a step toward her.

"Look here, in Latin, it says '*Veni Vidi Vici.*' I came, I saw, I conquered."

"That's a peculiar thing to have on a cigarette box."

He brushed his hair over to the side where it looked fuller.

"It's from Julius Caesar."

"Oh," she said, "that makes sense," and started to pack up her bag.

"I gotta go," she said. "I gotta go to work."

"Where do you work?"

"At a Xerox store. I gotta go."

"Wait," he said, feeling so vulnerable that his chin sank low pulling his mouth all the way open. "Don't you want to be friends?"

"I gotta go," she said. And so she did.

3

PETER

△△△

Peter felt all right stepping out of the smoky elevator, scorecard folded safely in his wallet. Kate was not the only one with a secret life. Sometimes he couldn't imagine how he had stood living with her for so long.

Their home was small, tidy and rent-controlled. They both cooked. Kate was better at it but he left the kitchen cleaner. When she did the wash she'd throw everything jumbled into a drawer. They both swept the floor, but only he mopped it. There was something in Kate's teeth that he still noticed. They were smoother than most and more blue.

Peter had looked closely at many women. Most actresses were light-conscious but not light-sophisticated. They wanted to be in the center of it without realizing how that concentrated visual energy transformed them. Most women had high expectations of pink. They thought it made them rosy and youthful like skillfully applied blush on the cheeks. When, in truth, it often gave a certain bloated flush like alcoholic emcees in a New Jersey strip club. Kate had started wearing lipstick on her thirtieth birthday and added a touch of black to her eyes some years after that. These are the little ways that one notices aging.

At first he didn't know what Kate's lover looked like. But some unfamiliar woman kept showing up at all of his wife's gallery openings and group shows without ever speaking to or looking at either of them. Finally he asked Spiros, Kate's art dealer, who that girl was and when Spiros answered, Peter was too surprised to be hurt. One day Kate had told him that she had a lover, that it was a woman and the woman's name. He had said "All right" and had since tried to ignore it. He had been busy with lots of projects and understood that Kate needed more attention. Since it was with a woman he didn't really mind, because as soon as he had more free time again, he'd expected Kate to break it off. Besides, there was something in the whole idea that was arousing. However, he'd never expected to have to contend with her physically. Certainly not with the fact that she was so awfully young. As soon as the surprise faded it was replaced by a sense of competition. He was jealous of Kate for having such a young lover.

The girl was listed in the phone book, listed very boldly with a full first name instead of that coy initial that most single women use to avoid obscene phone calls. That was how he learned that she lived two blocks away. If she and he were to stand on the roofs of their respective buildings, as he knew they had done on many sweltering summer nights, they could surely make out each other's silhouettes.

The next day Peter deliberately passed her place on the way to the gym and then stopped in front to look more closely. He saw her name on the intercom. It wasn't typed out neatly like the others, it was scrawled. Two names next to hers had been subsequently scratched out by different pens at different times.

She probably goes through lovers quickly, he thought, and decided to turn away just as she came walking down the block carrying a bag of groceries. He knew he shouldn't feel embarrassed. It was perfectly natural to be curious. Then he looked at her bags. They were overflowing. *She shops*, he thought, wanting to know everything about her.

When she saw Peter standing there waiting, her face went blank. She kept walking but he knew she was pretending. He knew she didn't want a confrontation. She didn't want anything to do with him at all.

Later on he decided that he did not mind so much when Kate snuck home in the middle of the night as long as she was always there when he woke up. That was the kind of unspoken courtesy that must exist between husband and wife. Peter knew that he had been driven to view Kate critically before seeing which structures were firmly in place between them. It was just as in nature, where one could more easily see what was brightly lit from a distance than when the viewer was illuminated on the spot. This was a fact of the natural world that made him want to proclaim a metaphor for human relations.

4

KATE

△△△

Rain made the day feel like night, but warmer and without threat.
When Kate walked along in the dark afternoon she could see
people sitting inside slightly illuminated restaurants. The ones
with the flattest colors reminded her of the old days when she
was a student in that very same neighborhood. Kate picked up
a *New York Times* and walked into a relic on the corner that still
had a lunch counter with a General Electric malted machine. In
the sixties that coffee shop had been considered overpriced, but
now it seemed comfortingly plain and ethnic, given what other
enterprises had erupted along the walkway. She opened the
paper, drank her coffee and then leaned back to stretch and look
around because the news was always the same.

At a small table was a red-haired man with a black woman
he really liked.

You don't see that so much anymore, Kate noted, remembering when interracial couples were a normal part of Greenwich

Village life. Nowadays there were a number of single older women, with gray frizzy hair and Jewish expressions, exhausted by their brown-skinned, up-to-date teenage children. Very few of those couples had stayed together. Of course, that could really be said about anyone who fell in love idealistically. Love with political implications had always interested her from a distance, but there was this ever present threat of violence accompanying it that she had managed, until now, to avoid.

The red-haired man at the next table liked the black woman he was with. He grinned when she talked to him and was pleased just to see her. She had spaghetti dreadlocks and a strawberry malt. Everyone in the place had different hair. There were two bald guys in old orange sweaters talking slowly in the corner because they'd known each other for a long time and could relax. There were a couple of aging punks drinking black coffee and some skinheads on skateboards buying ice cream.

It had been a hallucinatorily hot summer with AIDS wastes and other signs of the Apocalypse washing up on the beaches. Kate had spent it working in her studio, only in the evening, hoping to find some relief there. But she was still forced to cool off in the shower every hour and wear a T-shirt soaked in cold water before being able to concentrate on what she was making. One night she had heard many loud voices, as though someone had been shot or the drug dealers were arguing again. Then there was an incredible noise, a machine approaching like a war movie in Dolby sound. In the midst of what had been a hot, still night, the mess in her studio began to blow around the room because a helicopter hovered outside almost level with her windowframe. When it moved on, she stuck her head out all the way, leaned to the left and then saw crowds swarming. There were a lot of skinheads but also many regular neighbors plus punks and aging hippies. There were officers on the edges grabbing others arbitrarily and kicking them or hitting them with police sticks. It was more police in one place than Kate had seen since the sixties. It was real violence in the midst of great confusion. It was not a movie of the week. It was hot. It was stylized. It was unbelievable when it happened so openly. She stayed at the window watching and then made the decision not to enter into it.

She drank her second cup of coffee checking to be sure her purse was still tucked under the lunch counter. Now that it was September, that hot night had become a screen, another newscast, a spectacular event. It was the shred of an idea. Now, the same skinheads were buying ice cream in their sweatshirts, red bandannas and baggy army pants. Girls and boys with bleached blond military haircuts were hanging out again wearing T-shirts claiming I Survived the Tompkins Square Riot.

"Would you watch my raincoat while I go to the bathroom?" asked an earnest young woman clutching a notebook.

"Sure."

She returned quickly, slightly apologetic.

"I bought a new raincoat," she said, brushing it off with her fingers.

"It's a nice one," Kate said.

"It's crisp," the woman answered caressing the sleeves. "It's the first new coat that I've had in ten years. It fits. It's light for the summer and later, if it gets cold, I have a lining I can put in. The pockets won't have to be restitched every season. It zips."

She folded it carefully over the back of a chair.

"You know what scares me?" the woman said quietly like she was talking about the dead. "You look all around and know that it is the end of the empire. Then I look at myself and I have a new coat."

She was mousy, this woman, and a little bent over from too much scribbling in too many notebooks. Too much reading and not enough time in bed.

"When you get something new," she said conspiratorially, "you have to watch out that it doesn't get stolen. You have to avoid people who need money and people who need raincoats and keep them away from yours. But I feel bad being dry on the street when my brothers and sisters have nowhere to sleep."

"And contradictions are what let us know that we are fully human," Kate said.

"But?" the woman answered, waiting.

"But?"

"But," she said running old-looking hands over a young-looking face. "But then what?"

There were three or four things that terrified Kate and they came to her in moments, like the first sight of flamingo faces on the subway. Or, that pause after the nebulous closeness of love-making when the person's voice suddenly rang louder than all others. Kate feared the consequences of chaos but was comfortable with fragments, when they were freely chosen. In fact, she had lately been more excited by shreds of ideas and the partial phrases that paraded before her than in anything actually completed in her studio. But that did not worry her, because Kate had been making artwork long enough to recognize the patterns of frustration and breakthrough, denial and breakthrough, passion and frustration and breakthrough and change. Something was changing in the way she was seeing and it had started to affect her drawing.

KATE

△△△

Kate's last major stylistic shift had come four years earlier, when Spiros had put her on retainer and mounted her first successful solo show. She took in more money that season than Peter had in years of steady employment.

"You're using my ideas," he had complained. "You know there's no market for my work. No one can hang my work over a fireplace. Pure design challenges capitalism's view of the object. People always get rewarded for creating commodity products."

As he was speaking, Kate was looking sympathetically at his face. His lips were swollen and purple with wine as though they had been bruised. His face was covered by a thin slick of oily sweat. After years of being who he was and doing what he did, Peter's gestures had become a list of habitually repeated actions. Had her own as well? Years of the same expressions had turned his body into a collection of these shapes. But there was at the same time something endearing about his stubbornness, about

△△△ **15** his commitment to his art. She saw that he could be a fool or a hero, depending on how he was viewed. It was that quiet observation that had provoked Kate's switch to portraits.

She went straight from the coffee shop to her studio, letting the rain drip down her forehead and along the end of her nose. Without even taking off her coat, she went to a stack of old paintings and flipped through them impatiently. She wanted to smash them. She was tired of standing too far away from a person's face. She wanted to show what she saw making love or in a fight. It was a flash of lip, a pimpled cheek, sweat between the breasts, an unidentified slope or shadow that seemed suddenly more important. Sex and violence were sensual experiences, not visual ones, although they did have a visual component. In order to bring out the touch in the visual she had to get closer, as though her eye was on his chest looking up the side of his neck. That was where she wanted the image to be.

She opened her window wide and leaned out over the ledge, one hand grabbing the molding. The park had been quiet since the summer and was still green. There were thirty or forty make-shift shacks, tents, lean-tos serving as temporary shelter for at least 150 people. But no riots and very little noise from the police. Some stragglers had wrapped themselves in empty garbage bags while others just sat stoned and got soaked. The public bathroom was so overflowing with homeless people trying to stay dry that the crack smokers had to step over them to get inside.

Kate had never been homeless and she had never been hopelessly hungry. She had been mugged a number of times and raped once, years ago. She felt aware of the variety of violence she had both lived and missed and honored them all by clipping resonant images from papers and magazines, then taping them to her walls. There were black-and-whites of young Negro men being bitten by American police dogs. There were colored images of acknowledged heroes lying in swamps of their own blood. She searched each one for the particles of physicality that captured the fear, the pain and especially the willingness of some individual to enter into it. This was one aspect of what she meant by *chaos*. At times the sum of her collection drew such a repulsive conclusion that she couldn't imagine anything worse. But, looking out her window at the unprotected bodies, she considered that this worse thing was somehow present there.

On the side table by the single bed in her studio, Kate propped up a twenty-five-year-old photo from *Life* magazine. It showed a Buddhist monk who had set himself on fire in Saigon. The photo was one frame but it was all in motion. It caught the man at the point where he was so completely burned that his body crumpled over into the flame and flesh fell off his bones.

Does destroying yourself purposefully make a tangible impact?

What Kate retained from the photo of a collapsing human flame was a flash of light that put its faith in smoke and ashes.

6

KATE

△△△

Kate dialed Molly's number. She loved that she could call up
this younger woman and the woman wanted her. It was great.

"I miss you," Kate said into the phone. "I want to get together
soon."

Get together was her euphemism for making love.

Then Peter knocked on the door of her studio.

"I have to call you back," she said into the receiver. "Someone's walking in."

Peter wanted to know what he should pick up for dinner.

"I thought I'd get some sausages," he said.

"Okay, but get them at the new Italian place."

"I was thinking about Polish sausage."

"No, too greasy," she said. "Go to Rocco's, get some pasta
too. I'll make a sauce."

"Spinach pasta?" he asked.

"Or ravioli."

"I don't like ravioli," he said. "I think linguini would be better."

"What do you mean you don't like ravioli? You eat it all the time."

"That's true," he said. "But what about linguini?"

"Okay, fine, get that."

When he left, Kate dialed the number again.

"Okay."

"Okay."

"When are you free?" Kate asked, feeling flirtatious, fingering her lilacs. "Peter is going to be working tomorrow afternoon, so there's time between two and four, or are you working tomorrow?"

"I'm working until three. I could meet you then."

"No, Peter might stop by here at about a quarter after four."

"So, don't answer the bell, or tell him you have a date or you don't want to be disturbed. Tell him you're going to see me."

"What about Friday?"

"Listen, Kate, I have to talk to you about something." Kate could hear Molly straining to resist her seduction. "You saw me walking down the street Thursday and you pretended you didn't know who I was."

"I had to," Kate answered very quickly. "I was with Peter. You know that."

"Peter knows what I look like. I keep telling you. I found him standing outside my apartment the other day."

"It's irrelevant whether he does or not," Kate said worrying about Peter. "As long as he doesn't say anything about it to me, everything will be easier for all of us. I can't imagine me and Peter walking down the street and stopping to chat with you. It would be absurd."

"Look," Molly said, very calmly. "Last week you had your face between my legs and now you want to be there again."

"Don't you?" Kate said.

When she hung up the phone Kate sat quietly at the edge of her soft bed.

Of course, Molly had answered. *But I don't want to organize my fucking around Peter's schedule.*

Kate's bed had a fluffed feather comforter and matched clean sheets.

I just don't want to hurt his feelings, Kate thought. *I love him.*

There were dried tulip petals in a bowl surrounded by paint and fresh lilacs, so fragrant by her pillow.

What makes Peter so special is how smart he is, and how committed to his work. I admire that. I want to be able to have that much confidence, to believe so totally in what I am doing.

Peter was too large to sleep with her in that bed. They could make love but they couldn't sleep. Molly and she could sleep together quite comfortably there but they'd never had an entire night. Molly had a double bed at her house but the sheets were not as soft.

Molly had successfully insinuated herself right into the middle of Kate's habit of living and had then started agitating from the inside for change.

"Look," Molly had said. "If you want out, then get out now. If you want in, get in."

Kate knew exactly what Molly was trying to pull. And yet she felt surprisingly vulnerable to these frequent separations with threats of permanency. They pushed her into just enough panic to clarify what would be missing from her life without a girl-friend, without Molly specifically, with only Peter again. Molly had power over her. Molly forced Kate into symbolic concessions like eating dinner with her instead of with Peter and then making it up to him later, or more likely, eating twice. She always did give in eventually, which at first felt begrudging, but she got used to each step toward closeness and wondered if she was in over her head. No, she wasn't. Kate would never grant Molly free access, not in one lump sum and not piece by piece. It would never be that complete a relationship. On this point, Kate was certain.

Her hair was bright orange, naturally, and cut so close to her head that the strands stood up like bristles on a scrub brush. It was a buzz cut, exactly the kind Peter had worn as a little boy. She had seen it most recently on teenage girls and liked it in the mirror. Kate did not worry about being the only buzz-cut woman over forty in most public situations.

New Yorkers were not familiar with red hair. They didn't know how it worked. All they ever lived with was thick curly brown or straight black. Everything else was exotic. Red hair, blue eyes and red lips in New York made Kate a perpetual outsider except on Saint Patrick's Day. Old Jewish ladies stopped talking when she walked into the room. People always gave her directions even though she'd known where she was going for over twenty years.

Kate was a big woman with strong shoulders, sleek, and a neck of ivory. She could wear anything that black women wore; wild African prints, canary yellow and deep turquoise. Peter was her height and when they kissed they were eyeglass to eyeglass. Molly was much shorter and had to stretch to reach her mouth. Was that why she kissed Kate's neck so much?

"I always knew I would get to a woman eventually," she had confided to Spiros, sitting over coffee one late afternoon in the back of his gallery. "But I could never picture precisely how. I couldn't imagine growing apart from Peter or any of the horrible scenes that would have to take place to separate us."

"Are you two fighting?" he asked carefully.

"No," she said. "There is a silent tolerance."

"So continue with them both forever."

"If she will allow it."

"Well," Spiros said, rolling his lips back between a smile and a purse. "Can you and this girl have a future?"

"With Molly so many things could go wrong. She'd get bored or want to eat me up. She wouldn't leave me any free time. She'd trap me, try to turn me into a lesbian. I wouldn't be able to do my artwork if I was with her."

"Why not?"

"Because . . . she's not intellectual enough."

"Well then, it is clear," he said. "Good to be sure about that."

"Why?"

"Because, Kate. If you are going to invest in the past you'd better end up choosing the past. If you give priority to the past, don't find yourself in the future. Waiting for you there will be a very angry young woman."

"I never know, Spiros, whether you are threatening me or just giving friendly advice."

"All right, I won't tell you anything more. You tell me. If you were going to name a sonnet after Molly, what would you call it?"

" 'Six Lines of Enjoyment.' "

"But a sonnet has fourteen lines . . . oh, I understand."

Even as a teenager Kate had never spent so much time kissing on the street as she did now, leaning into Molly's mouth against a parked car. She found her body pressed against all kinds of surfaces as these public kisses began to span seasons. There were barstools and doorways, bare patches of rare grass in a few straggly parks. And always a longing refuge in her lover's body.

When they couldn't meet at night they kissed in the late afternoon and made love and were outside again kissing by dusk. Then she had to go meet Peter, usually to get to the theater. Most evenings of every week she and Peter sat next to each other in an audience. She was not the kind of woman who wanted to sit alone. She wanted to sit with him. Then they would have something to talk about at night; what they had just seen. Kate would be so lonely without someone sitting next to her agreeing.

Some nights in an audience Kate felt happy because she and her lover had just embraced. Sometimes that made her warm and loving toward Peter because his silence permitted her this pleasure. She'd slide her arm around his and pull him closer to her knowing that any show of affection lulled him into a happy contentment. Sometimes, though, she'd feel lost in Molly and indifferent to her husband, for which she'd compensate immediately with much direct attention. Two relationships, she'd noticed, required the constant application of triage. But mostly, the transition from Molly to Peter was natural.

Kate looked down at her toes. They were clean. Her toenails were trimmed. The hair was red around her ankles, so light it didn't need to be shaved. Her eyelashes were pale orange, like an evening sun, and long enough to dust her face. She always kept the hair under her arms clipped with a small scissor hanging over the sink for that purpose. She and Peter looked good together aesthetically.

He was sweet from the first time they met. At that time he was a girl. His face was smooth, anyway, for a man, but Kate used to dress him up in girl's clothing. She'd put him in panties. They'd laugh and he'd prance around twisting his hips like a fag. She'd put her fingers on the lace and feel his dick underneath. He was not afraid to dress that way. He knew who he was. He was a girl.

"Peter's such a girl," Kate would say to Molly every now and then.

"What do you mean?"

"He's a baby. He's passive. He whines and can't take care of himself. He never carries the heaviest thing."

"That's not like a girl," Molly said, that annoyed tone in her voice. "That sounds exactly like a man to me. I hate when you say things like that. You're not thinking for yourself. You're just repeating something you heard. Just because Peter isn't brutal doesn't automatically make him a hero, you know."

"What are you talking about?"

Kate thought about something else then. She had no intention of engaging this kind of thinking. She thought about some other different thing.

"How come you never had children?" Molly had asked her one afternoon as they were kissing by the water in East River Park.

It had to do with her family, but it seemed like too much to go into right then.

"I had one of those families," Kate said, looking for an entertaining detail that would explain them without too much effort, "where we all had first names beginning with the same letter. Kathleen, that's me, Kelly, Kevin, Kerry was my sister who died, and Keith. We had pillow fights and breakfasts and went to Latin mass on Sundays. My mother was a dentist. The only time she ever touched us was when she worked on our teeth. My dad was more fun, a drinker, a businessman, a little more intimate."

"Doesn't sound too bad."

"No, Molly, it wasn't bad, it's just that I grew up in America and every time I think about having my own kids, I remember that they would have to live there too and be young Americans for at least twenty years. That's when I decide no.''

"That's not my America," Molly said, leaning over the railing into gray-green-white smoke backgrounds. "I had one of those families where my mother would say 'Children in Brooklyn are starving' and my father would say 'Yeah, starving.' He always had some friend sleeping on the sofa because my parents could not say no. When I marched in the gay pride march my mother said 'You wear your problems like a banner on Fifth Avenue.' And my father said 'Yeah, Fifth Avenue.' ''

"When you think back on all that, how does it seem to you?" Kate asked.

"Old-fashioned," Molly said. "But so am I. That's why I don't want children."

"I don't understand," Kate said, moving closer. "Being Mom is the most old-fashioned thing a woman can do."

"But," Molly answered, taking her hand as they walked along, "it also means entering fully into the modern world. I don't want certain things in my life like computers, pop stars or TV shows. I choose oblivion to all that. With children, the outside world becomes unavoidable unless you isolate them completely."

"In which case," Kate added, "they'd end up totally helpless to defend themselves against a nation of monsters raised on Tang. Besides, I feel like I already have a husband and a child or a mistress and a son or a mother and a father but mostly two children."

"Shows what kind of parent you would be."

"What's that supposed to mean? That I would seduce my own daughter?"

Kate was surprised by the matter-of-fact perversity that had crept into her conversation but then felt pleased at being able to express it so easily.

"Listen," Molly said. "You do not have a maternal relationship to me. I'm your lover. I'm just younger. But you don't take care of me, so don't pretend that you do."

When Molly spoke to her that way, Kate didn't want to listen.

She heard the challenge, imagined the reason and knew enough to let it go at that. It didn't mean that her feelings never changed. They did, but not because Molly said they should. So the tensions continued, slightly under the surface. This one was resolved some months later in an afternoon when they were ready for love.

"Kate, take my earrings out for me, will you? I don't feel like doing it for myself."

Kate felt the silver slide through Molly's ear, casting shapes on her neck like Indonesian shadow puppets. Then the pieces of metal were lying still in her palm. Kate surprised herself by thinking, *How could two women ever be closer than this?* Later she realized it wasn't so much a sudden closeness but that she had grown to love Molly. She hadn't loved her at first, but she did now.

"What are you thinking about?" Molly asked.

"Thinking about you."

"What about?"

"That you are becoming more real to me."

"Good," Molly said, holding her, holding her head against Kate's chest, so girly and soft. "Now I don't have to be your child anymore. From now on I'll be your mistress."

It didn't feel like a threat.

7

PETER

△△

All summer, every single person had been uncomfortable. It was not unusual for the city to smell of baking garbage and decomposing bodies. But most New Yorkers found a point each season when they begrudgingly accepted the heat. They no longer tried to defy it. They picked out the air-conditioned subway cars, knew which banks to stop in to cool off between the subway and work. They slowed down their pace of accomplishment in order to accommodate it. But this summer had been different. There had been a suffocating brutality that seemed brand-new. It was the absolute lack of relief that put each person into a private state of wondering if it would ever get cool again. This year Peter noticed that the air had stayed so warm there was a creeping sensation of melting polar ice caps and a lot of speculation about the greenhouse effect as *seasons* came to an end as a concept.

Peter was past forty and intended to live as long as possible. He took care of his body, but more importantly, he had developed an approach, a way of facing the world that left him enough room to breathe. He never scheduled one event on top of another, so there was always extra time to do new things on a whim, like run that strip of land along the Hudson River where developers were demolishing the piers.

It is so important to have flat, open space by the waterfront, he thought, inhaling the salt. It was the only place a man could go to get between the city and the sea.

All along the route someone had spray-painted the word *Justice* inside stencils of pink triangles. He wondered if that was just another rock band, but then got lost in the feeling of the open city over his left shoulder and the sea breeze on his right. He was having a good run until the air between him and water started to get more complicated and cluttered with the beginnings of various constructions. There were ditches, then pipes and strips of metal until, surprisingly, there was no more water at all. Instead he came upon an incongruous addition to the island of Manhattan. It was stuck on like some clumsy extension or unsightly tumor that had grown where the borough was once sleek and symmetrical.

The sign said:

Welcome to Downtown City
Ronald Horne, Developer

Then he remembered from his newspaper reading that this was created land. It was invented real estate. He had recently skimmed an article about this in *The New York Times* business section. Manhattan was running out of property, so Ronald Horne had extended it by filling in the water around the island, piece by piece. Eventually a person would be able to walk to New Jersey and Ronald Horne would collect the toll. In the meantime, Peter decided, he'd better keep on top of zoning laws if he wanted a grasp on his own future.

Downtown City's main drag was called Freedom Place. That was the perfect name for this morally slipshod era—meaninglessly patriotic and so crass. The buildings were mostly sky-rise condominiums, although there were a few newly constructed waterfront townhouses reminiscent of Henry James's Washington Square. That way the truly wealthy could stare out at Ellis Island through their bay windows as they drank down their coffee every morning. The only visible storefront was Chemical Bank.

Peter jogged past the playground filled with black maids watching white children, past the stretch limos and sportier imports. But when he got to Liberty Avenue he just had to stop and stare. There were two huge brand-new office buildings of identical design with their names emblazoned in gold: New York Realty and United States Software. These were Ronald Horne's largest and most profitable holdings, according to all the profiles and interviews Peter had seen of the billionaire. The guy was on TV more often than Walter Cronkite. Was Walter Cronkite still on TV? Looking around him at all that wealth, Peter saw immediately how Downtown City was advanced capitalism's version of the company town. It was like those snowy corners of the Northwest that he'd passed through on tour, where the Wallace Company Store was on Wallace Avenue and everyone worked at the Wallace Mine which all added up to Wallace, Idaho. Only, in this case, Downtown City was a huge barracks for investment bankers. Even though the complex had only recently been inaugurated, Liberty Avenue was designed to replicate the solid turn-of-the-century Rockefeller-style riches usually found on Fifth. There was a square, pre-Depression, old-money austerity; an impenetrable magnificence. No expense had been spared and yet there was nothing garish; imported marble, tasteful ironwork, elegant windows. It had all the elements of a made-to-order American shrine.

It is design machismo, Peter thought, deciding to share this observation with Kate later. It is intimidation architecture. He had to be sure to tell her that one too.

Peter ran on through Battery Park past all the signs warning of rat poison and past all the homeless people avoiding the lines of tourists waiting to see the Statue of Liberty. He sprinted through the South Street Seaport, Manhattan's only shopping mall, down around the big Pathmark where every morning black men and old Chinese women in straw hats stood together on line waiting to cash in the empty cans they had collected for the five-cent deposit. The river smelled of abandoned cars, old fish and stale beer. Peter turned up East River Park, under the Manhattan Bridge, and jogged slowly back over to the West Side. That morning, everything had been white; his T-shirt, his jock, shorts, socks and running shoes. Now they were soaked in his sweat and covered in the city's filth. He was happy. He was a dirty, sweaty man.

He stopped in a restaurant for an iced tea, and leaned back in the booth, feeling his blood pulse. At the next table were two young men, overdressed in fashionable new wave suits and short haircuts showing clean necks with equally pristine ties.

"Look, you stop talking about Rick and I'll stop talking about the goddamn cat."

Peter watched them whine like two suburban matrons. He hated to see men act like that. No, he corrected himself, he hated when anyone acted like that. A third man joined them then, just as overdressed and just as slight. Peter noticed that his own chest was twice the size of theirs.

"There you are, did you find them?"

"Yes I did," the newcomer snapped, tired and annoyed. "Here you go."

He dumped a pile of black ribbons onto the table, then picked out one to wrap around his upper arm, finally extending it for a companion to fasten.

"I tried to tie it on myself," he said. "But I couldn't get the ribbon to lie flat. Will you pin it?"

8

PETER

Peter drank down his tea and thumbed through a discarded copy of *New York* magazine. The Horne family was featured on the cover seated around a bountiful dinner table. The men all had oversize heads with receding blond hairlines and Quasimodo postures. There were huge portions on their plates.

Some art director's idea of political commentary, thought Peter. The women were uniformly thin-lipped over plates of diverse lettuce. They smiled, watching their husbands eat.

"We have a close family," Horne told the reporter. "My children never have to make appointments to see me."

On the next page Horne was in the backseat of his limo talking on the phone and printing out on his mobile fax machine.

"Private sector," he said. "That's the future. The whole city should be run by businessmen. I could do a much better job with the prison system than any government official. I'd love to buy the prison system and show New York how to treat its criminals.

And my attorneys have assured me that having a monopoly on crime does not violate any antitrust laws. It just has to do with your definition of trust."

Peter closed the magazine, replacing it neatly underneath the umbrella stand. He looked through the coffee shop window at some goings-on at the church across the way. It was a large crowd that morning, a somber one. Many of the men were wearing suits but some were more relaxed, in tasteful white slacks or light prints. Even the pallbearers lifting the casket out of the hearse had something very casual about them.

I would never wear white to a funeral, Peter thought. Some of the men had ponytails, others were more normal. The women were somehow not as attractive as the men. Not that, exactly, they just weren't as well dressed.

Something is not right here, he thought. Only then did Peter realize that the men were arriving alone or with each other, in couples and groups. The women came in couples or with men they couldn't possibly be involved with.

This is gay, he thought. *This is a homosexual church.*

Then he realized that it was not a homosexual church, but a Catholic one, filled with homosexuals. He watched them walking up the white marble staircase, preparing to mourn.

Ever since Kate had begun her gay affair Peter had been slapped in the face by homosexuality practically every day. How ironic that her affair had coincided with this AIDS thing. It was like running into someone he hadn't thought about for years and then seeing them coincidentally three times a week until the recognition became an embarrassment. Peter had always been around gay men—being in the theater, how could he avoid it? Not that he wanted to avoid it, of course. Anyway, most technicians tended to be straight except for the women. But he had to admit that his and Kate's inner circle were all heterosexual couples. It had just turned out that way. Some of the men he knew had been bisexual at one time, but those experiments were all over now, he noted with some relief. Now things were more clearly defined.

Peter had once had a gay affair. It was with a master electrician named Carl Jacobs. Carl was twenty years older and had taken him on as an apprentice. When Peter worked with someone closely he always fell in love. It was part of being in theater. When the show was over they would rarely see each other again, but that distance wasn't resented. It was normal. Carl's hair was completely white and his face was wrinkled. He had a purely white beard, trimmed but full, and white hair poked out of the top of his shirt. They had worked together like guys work; quietly, no gossip, just moving their bodies at the right times and understanding each other's rhythms. They took very good care of each other, running errands, sharing cigarettes and barely talking.

When it was time to focus and they were finally down to the last light, Carl came and stood next to him. Peter could feel the old man's body heat with his torso, and the heat of the light with his hands.

"Would you move that slightly upstage please, darling?" Carl said with a quiet growl.

At the word *darling*, Peter took his hands from the electricity and put them on Carl's soft, soft face, kissing his mouth. He was meaty and large compared to Kate or any woman. There was something to hold on to. They pressed their bodies against each other's and Peter felt his cock get hard against Carl's. It was such a beautiful feeling; two men and two cocks, both scented and of the same mind. When Peter tried to blow Carl, the old man's dick swelled in his mouth and Peter gagged on it, feeling a sour spit rising in his throat.

"That's all right," Carl said kindly. "Use your hands."

Then they sat naked next to each other on the stage eating sandwiches, not talking. Peter sat there smelling him, looking at his cock against his thigh, looking at the old man's eyes and the veins in his legs. Then Carl turned to him and said, "You are not just lighting the action and the image. You are lighting the voices. You give them light to hear by. What could be more subtly defined than differing dimensions of air?"

After paying the restaurant check, Peter decided that he wanted to be around gay people more. Kate was probably spending more time with them and he wanted to, too. It would bring them closer together. That's what had been troubling him all week, actually. Kate and that woman had clearly had a fight. He could tell from the pained expression she tried to hide. She was sour sometimes, with a particular distaste that only comes from longing for a lover. He was honestly curious to hear the details, to know the scenario of their fight and separation, to comfort her. But after having fully imagined Kate's tearful confidence about her lost girlfriend, he realized that such an event would reduce his stature in her eyes to that of friend or brother and not the husband he was determined to be. It was better to wait patiently for Molly to simply disappear. Then Peter decided to go into the church.

The huge marbled ceilings made it cooler inside. It was cool but the air was still. Peter stayed in the back because he was a tourist, and had learned from traveling in Mexico that when you are watching another culture in church it is best to stand in the back. There was music coming from the balcony but it wasn't the organ he had expected. Instead a harpsichord was being played. Perhaps the dead man had been a harpsichord fan. Peter guessed that homosexuals were probably as creative with their funerals as they were with everything else. But after a while he found the instrument's tone annoying. Pounding was half the sound and much too abrasive for a funeral. He inhaled the incense and felt again how still the air was. It barely circulated. The smell was beginning to be overpowering, stifling actually. Peter felt faint and sat down abruptly in the nearest pew. Even though he tried repeatedly to relax, he just couldn't breathe. His lungs would not fill with air, so he left as quietly and respectfully as he had come, stepping back into an almost oppressive heat, only able to take a full deep breath a few blocks away.

When he got back to the apartment late that afternoon, Kate had just returned from the studio and had brought home her coveralls to be washed. They were laid out over the dresser next to a bag of groceries that hadn't been put away. She had started changing into more attractive clothing but had gotten waylaid by something real or imagined and seemed halfway about everything. As Peter watched her, he noticed with a quiet sadness how Kate could be euphoric or depressed for no visible reason. All week she'd been irritable, waiting for something, or teary-eyed and deeply regretful. He had actually caught her a few times staring out the window as she was doing at this moment. He stood watching her. The muted sunlight brought out only the surface texture of her face and so he saw every wrinkle and crack in the skin. He saw how her hair would look when it turned white and her features, how they would fall. Then, in one calm and graceful motion, she turned her eyes like the girl in the Vermeer painting being interrupted at her music lesson. The slight twist of her neck and the engagement of her eyes presented themselves with a candor that was always flirtatious. Now that her affair was over and had clearly ended badly, Peter knew that only he could make her happy again.

9
MOLLY

△△△

Molly was glad her bed was warm and the night hot because she carried with her a faint but present desire to masturbate to Kate. She thought *to her* as if it were a gift, but she actually meant to masturbate *to* a memory of making love with her like one moves *to* a piece of music.

She was in a hallucinatory state. It was too hot and her body could not get cool. Each part of her was sore and had a distinct odor. When Kate said "I love you," its effects lingered on Molly's skin like radiation. Molly could sail out the window on the strength of that alone. She could fly out into the sky that was always between her apartment and Kate's like an ocean of buildings instead of barnacles. When Molly sat on the bed and looked out the window she could just make out the shadow of terra cotta surrounding Kate's rooftop.

"I want to be a good lover to you," Molly said to the gray-red funnels and chimneys, the slanted collapsing mountains that formed the boundaries of their pleasureland.

"But I want you to be a good lover to me as well. I want this to be reciprocal."

Molly lived with this conflict like an itch, like mites laying eggs under the skin that made her squirm with discomfort, especially at night, when she, without restraint, relived those moments of pure anger. Like waiting for Kate. She seemed to always be waiting, the afternoon getting longer and later until it disappeared into that other time. Then a figure would appear, finally, on the stairs preceded by huge flowers. Molly was immediately reduced to some businessman's daughter whose daddy tried to replace a forgotten birthday with a gift too large and obvious to have any meaning.

"I couldn't leave on time because Peter was hanging around. I would have had to say where I was going."

"You should have told him you had an appointment with me and had to leave."

At the same time that she spoke, Molly thought about having to watch those flowers wilt and crumble all over the floor before Kate came back to her again.

Maybe someday she'll come while the last bunch is still fresh, Molly thought. *If she does that, I'll sprinkle the petals on her chest.*

She dialed Kate's number. The phone rang. It rang again and Molly decided not to hang up because she liked knowing the room it was ringing in, having memories in that room. But after a dream that lasted five rings she heard the click that announced the presence of an answering machine, to be followed one breath later by a greeting, perhaps accompanied by music. That was new. Kate had bought an answering machine for her studio. Who wanted to come home to messages? Molly had long ago decided that buying an answering machine would be a public admission of a private sin; waiting for women to call her. It made her rush home from work to sit next to the phone, refusing even to go out for a newspaper. Phone machines were an announcement to the world that a person wanted more calls than they were getting. They thought there was actually more attention out there trying to get through. Who wanted to confirm the nothing behind the fantasy? She's not really calling you. Besides, those machines changed the way people communicated. It's so much less personal than a direct call. There was something provocative and challenging about another person's voice entering, uninvited, into your home at any moment.

Then again, maybe Kate's machine was a personal message to her estranged lover, an open door saying "I want to know what you have to say." Besides, some people gave up if they couldn't get in touch.

Molly hung up the receiver without saying a word. She couldn't take the chance. A minute later, regretting that decision, she dialed again. But, having forgotten to practice a message, hung up one more time. That was one of the dangers of those machines. Once left, the message was out of your control and could never be taken back.

This was how it always unfolded. Molly looked for reasons to capitulate because she loved Kate and wanted to be with her. But she hated having to accommodate Peter. He was a straight man. Molly was a gay woman. Why should she have to take care of him? So, Molly just waited for the day when Kate would find it unacceptable to say "I'm going to the store" when she was going to her. Maybe she could learn to act like Peter and exert silent control. Don't *ask* for anything. Just expect it. For Peter this process came so naturally he could never be accused of malicious intent. That was his strategic advantage over her. It was called *normal*.

Molly knew what her own apartment must look like from the outside; empty, yellow, stark. Alone inside the box her morality was slipping. There was a hot breeze, but it was still a breeze, coming in through the window, and she was planning how to behave. She was so hurt. The only salve was an extended imagining of what she could have if she ever became a full person in the world.

I would choose her presence, Molly thought. *Followed by a quiet spontaneity.*

10
MOLLY

△△

What did Molly imagine sitting there that way? She saw the ghost of this woman reclining demurely on the couch with outstretched feet. So, Molly stretched hers out as well and ran her hand over the light red hairs on those spider legs. The woman was saying something from a perspective Molly would never have considered on her own but could now predict from repeated exposures. Then she noticed again how truly beautiful Kate was. Her arms carried carefully defined muscles that she used for texture as she moved. At their first meeting she had been tall and proper, a feminine tomboy like Nancy Drew's best girlfriend, George. She discussed things with her forefinger sitting in the cleft of her chin. Her eyes looked her age.

The second time Molly saw her she was naked in the locker room of a neighborhood pool. Her eyes came up to Kate's breasts, which were small with no weight. Kate's nipples and her lips were the same color, a pale peach, like tiger lilies. Almost every part of her body reminded Molly of flowers, vibrant colors found only in nature. She could see how carefully Kate's body was constructed, how much she stood out physically being so tall, with hair so short it left her ears and neck available to anyone. Molly wanted to keep her talking and give her something to remember so she launched into a story about a writer named Jane, and her Moroccan lover who cast spells against her until she was so confused she could no longer form coherent speech.

"But how do you know?" Kate said, effusive, meeting Molly's enthusiasm, engaging it. "How do you know it was Cherifa who stopped her?"

Molly answered leaning against the wet, white tiles. She chose her words carefully, their hair and skin smelling of sweat and hot chlorine.

"If you love someone very much and they want to destroy you, that is enough to destroy you."

"Yes it is," she said. "It certainly is."

That was their first communication. Both women had been, at least once, destroyed.

Gestures and snippets of their courtship stood out more clearly than complete conversations. One night, on the way home from somewhere, Kate stopped suddenly to take Molly's face in her hand and draw flaming red lipstick on her mouth with the other.

"I don't understand how you can live on three days of work a week."

"I can," Molly said. "I have a rent-controlled apartment. I don't buy anything. I don't eat out."

"Okay, you don't go to the opera, but a person cannot survive taking tickets at a movie theater part-time, not in the consumer age."

"I'm not a consumer. Look, I don't have a stereo so I don't buy records or cassettes. I buy regular food like eggs. I don't have to pay for organic quinoa. I buy books on the street. Yesterday I found *The Heart Is a Lonely Hunter* for fifty cents. I obviously don't buy clothes."

But Kate was so convinced that Molly needed a higher standard of living that she started finding her bartending jobs at gallery openings and various private parties, where she could make salary and tips and take home leftover Brie at the end of the night.

It wasn't long before Molly was employed as a servant for one of Spiros's parties. Kate came and stood very close to her a few times and Molly poured, wiped and stared at Kate while she danced. She watched Kate move, and after some wine, Kate began to move for her. She came closer still and then left with her husband. That was Molly's first sharp sensation of unjust abandonment. She wondered sincerely for the rest of the night if Kate always wanted to leave at precisely the same moment he did. Or was it that no moment was worth experiencing once he was absent from it? Yet, at the same time she felt a certain exhilaration because that was such a beautiful way to communicate with another person, watching her dance.

Kate had called the next evening. They had chatted. She called again the night after that. They chatted again. She called the third night, which was the Fourth of July. The fireworks started at twenty after nine, but Molly had stayed inside her hot apartment because she knew that Kate would call her.

"What are you doing?"

Molly waited a breath before answering.

"Come over," she said.

Molly didn't change her clothes. She was short and sweaty and hot. Her shirt was too small and her shorts were baggy. She stank. Kate stood in the doorway and after two shy moments they placed their lips dryly on each other's mouths. Kate was tall. She had red eyelashes and wore a shirt with beige tongues on it. They sat on the roof while things were exploding. Molly was so happy she couldn't speak. She couldn't explain anything or answer any questions. She didn't want to talk. She wanted to be really romantic.

"Can I kiss you?" she said. "Let's kiss."

Kate was sitting then. Molly was standing, so she held Kate's head in her hands and kissed her. Kate laughed then, putting her long arms around Molly's shoulders, and said, "You're fresh."

"Then she said, "This is a strange night. There are pinwheels of firecrackers, spinning and spitting with bursts of gunfire. Emotions explode on a night like this."

Molly had never been called *fresh* before. It was a completely new word. What did it mean? She kissed Kate's neck, running her fingers back and forth over the bristles of Kate's haircut. She loved her. Kate was a boy. She was shy and looked down without saying what she was thinking.

"How do you feel, Kate?"

"Not sure," she said. "I go very slowly in matters of this nature."

"I go very quickly."

Molly knew, of course, that she did not go very quickly but it was obviously the most romantic thing to say. What was she supposed to do, tell the truth and admit to being a nerd? She was, after all, trying to convince a married woman to fall into bed with her and then roll around there for a while.

They stood at the door again, molding their hands into each other's, and Molly watched Kate come in to kiss her. Kate turned her neck to both sides, like a soft wave, but in slow motion with her eyes closed. Everything was light orange then, when her lowered lids blocked out the ice blue of her eyes. She was plain. She was effeminate, like a beautiful faggot. Lips in place, they kissed. Even though Molly bit her mouth and licked her neck and grabbed handfuls of muscle from her arms, Kate didn't move. Molly was excited then and embarrassed and so hopeful and invested.

"Will I see you again?" she asked and immediately forgot the answer.

"Come back," Molly said as Kate walked out her door.

"I will," she said, but it was a lie.

Molly called her for two months. She left messages under the door of Kate's studio saying she would be home by eight, that she was taking tickets at Cinema Village and could get Kate into *Godfather II* for free. Sometimes Kate answered the phone but said she was busy and couldn't talk. Still, Molly persevered because the one thing Kate never said was "Don't call me, I don't want to see you."

In fact, Kate often said she would call back as soon as she

wasn't busy. But she never did. She lied instead. So, Kate's lack of definition became constant fodder for Molly's firm belief in everyone's potential for change, and she continued despite the odds. She was willful. She was desiring. She was very deliberate. Molly decided to change her approach. She stopped calling. She stopped slipping messages under the door. She stopped reading Kate's horoscope. Instead she sent a very careful letter.

"I held the envelope in my hand," Kate told her later. "With slight distaste I opened it, expecting to find some unpleasant adolescent cajole, some threat or wail. It was going to take an unimportant example of poor judgment and turn it into a major event. It would make you more important, Molly, than I intended for you to be because fighting with someone is very, very intimate. Tolerating them is condescending but being angry at someone is the best way of keeping them in your life."

They sat across a table from each other as Kate said this. There was little communication and not much light. Molly felt cold on the top of her skin and very still underneath.

"When you are angry at someone, they are present. You have something to be mad at, you have them. Then they have to consider you. They have to have an opinion. I opened the letter. It said, 'bluish carmine, velvety.' That's when it all began, of course."

11

MOLLY

△△△

It was very hot that evening, so most people wore shorts and light tank tops. There was a lot of white. There were white balloons on strings, one for every friend who had died. At the beginning of the route people handed out magic markers and passed them along, so each one could write the names of their friends on the balloons. Some people had one balloon. Some people had eight. Some had more. A few were carefully inscribed with detailed information like "Thomas Ho 1957–1987." Others just said "Ray." People also held white candles, which gave the anxious something to fuss about, like keeping it lit or catching the wax. Men and women smiled and said quiet soft hellos or kept to themselves. Mostly they just walked down the street. There was not much sound, in the way that New York can be a silent city against a backdrop of solid noise. Molly looked over the balloons and read the names. She carried two of her own. She saw the name of someone she had known peripherally and hadn't even realized was sick.

By the time they got to the river many of the marchers were dripping sweat from their necks. Drops were sliding down their temples. Everyone stopped then and was even more quiet than before. Each person looked at the water, how dirty it was, how much garbage was floating in it. They looked across to the Jersey side, at the high rises in Fort Lee and the polluted mess that made up the rest of it. Each one had a very private thought about a person who had died or about themself or about New Jersey or why they weren't feeling anything right then. It was the calmest state of confusion that Molly had ever been in. Then somebody started to sing. When that man made the first sound he startled the other mourners, who felt interrupted. But after the second note every single person who had come to the AIDS vigil realized that the man was singing "somewhere over the rainbow." Another man let his balloons fly off over the water and one by one as they were singing "somewhere over the rainbow," other people let their balloons fly away. Molly looked out at the water and the reddish industrial-waste sunset and thought two thoughts. She watched the balloons rising toward the filthy sky and thought, *They leave your hand the way they leave your life.* She could only really see the sea of them after losing sight of her own. Then she thought, *bluish carmine, velvety.*

What does it mean to sing "somewhere over the rainbow" and release balloons? It made her feel something very human; a kind of nostalgia with public sadness and the sharing of emotions. But then what?

To a certain extent she had gotten used to hearing about people dying. She hadn't gotten used to seeing it, but now when someone said, "I couldn't call you back because a friend of mine died," it was said calmly.

This dying had been going on for a long time already. So long, in fact, that there were people alive who didn't remember life before AIDS. And for Molly it had made all her relations with men more deliberate and detailed. First, the men changed. They were more vulnerable and open and needed to talk. So she changed. Passing acquaintances became friends. And when her friends actually did get sick there was a lot of shopping to do, picking up laundry and looking into each other's eyes. She had never held so many crying men before in her life.

Molly had recently spent three months cooking dinner for a man who was so disoriented he couldn't decide how to cut the spinach. His name was on one of her balloons. There were drugs that he wanted to try but the Food and Drug Administration wouldn't approve them.

"I'm dying," he said before the dementia set in. "Let me take the goddamn drug."

The best he could find was a placebo program where half the men got sugar pills and the other half got experimental drugs. No one knew who got what.

"Why do they need a comparison study?" he said to everyone. "They already know what happens if you don't treat it."

He didn't say that to the doctors though, because he was afraid that if he made trouble they would give him sugar instead of medicine.

He got old very fast. He said the telephone was on fire. His skin broke open. His mother came in from Saint Louis and kissed his face when it was covered with sores. He went to the hospital and then he went home. Then he went to the hospital. Then he went home. Then he went to the hospital. Then he died in the hospital.

Molly knew this man, Ronnie Lavallee 1954–1987, because his sister Cecilia was a dyke who used to work with Molly at an all-women's trucking company that delivered gay male pornography. Since she had a gay brother, the two women used to stop by his place after work sometimes to drink beer and bring him free stroke books. One day when Cecilia was at karate camp, Molly and Ronnie were sitting in his living room watching Paul Morrissey's *Trash* on his VCR. They were eating Chinese food and drinking Chinese beer. On the TV Joe Dallesandro was a junkie who couldn't get a hard-on but didn't really care and was still beautiful. His girlfriend was Holly Woodlawn, the drag queen, and her sister and ex-lover was played by a pregnant, naked Viva.

"I love this movie," Ronnie said. "It is the greatest acting in any movie except for Valerie Perrine in *Lenny*."

Then he said, "Molly, would you look at this?" and he lifted up his shirt like a little boy asking his mommy to look at his tummy.

"What is it?" he said.

"That looks like a mole to me," she said. "How long have you had it?"

"Four weeks."

"Well," she said, remembering when her other friend Joseph DeCarlo 1960–1982 had his face covered with splotches. "I've seen lesions and they're usually raspberry, I think. I've never seen a brown one before and this is brown."

Molly sat back relieved. But Ronnie had an expression on his face that she had never seen on any face before.

"What about this one?" he said, pulling up his pants leg.

It was red.

Molly really wanted to say that it didn't look like a lesion, that it didn't look like Kaposi's sarcoma, that it didn't look like AIDS, but it did.

"I don't want to die," he said.

Later on in the hospital he said, "I don't intend to die." He looked her in the eye. "Not everyone dies. Michael Callen is still alive."

But she saw doubt so she knew.

After the dementia set in he said the telephone was on fire. He got so emaciated that Molly couldn't recognize him. He got so disoriented he couldn't recognize his sister or his old boyfriend or his nurse. That's when Molly stopped visiting the hospital.

When everyone felt that the vigil was over they started looking at each other and drifting into small groups for talk and comfort before walking home through the hot city in early-night light. Molly felt enormous anger. These were her friends. These were her dead friends. She saw their faces. Were their lives worth less than the lives of heterosexuals? Where was Kate? She should be there at a time like this.

As she turned up the street away from the water, Molly saw

two men handing out leaflets. That was not the first thing she noticed about them. The first thing she saw was that they were wearing black T-shirts. On their chests were large pink triangles with the word *Justice* scrawled, graffiti style. She wished she had a girlfriend she could go to and hold and tell the story of the day, but she didn't, so Molly sat down instead on the hood of a parked car and watched the two men distribute their papers.

The shirts were angry but the men were smiling. The older one was black. He wore his hair in a large natural like Angela Davis used to do, which made him look distinctly old-fashioned. No one wore their hair that way anymore. It was either clean-cut or Grace Jones or dreadlocks. But this guy reminded Molly immediately of those posters of Huey P. Newton sitting on a throne holding machine guns. Only this man wasn't wearing a black beret and leather jacket. Instead he had on effeminate floral-print three-quarter pants like girls buy on Fourteenth Street. He had a gold loop and a ruby stud in one ear and a feather in the other. He was swish. He was an older black gay man who called other men "darling" and "girlfriend." On the center of each flower printed on his pants was the word *love*.

"Here, handsome, take this please. You know I only want what's best for you."

The second man was much younger and taller and white. He had a long ponytail and good teeth. Then Molly got off the car and took a leaflet.

DO YOU THINK IT'S RIGHT?
That people are dying and the government does nothing? If you do not think that this is right then do something about it.

The flyer went on to invite people to a weekly meeting. Molly folded it four times and pushed it into her pocket. She missed Kate very much. She wished Kate were there. Molly walked home feeling open and vulnerable and then very angry with an energy that had nowhere to go.

12
KATE

△△△

She hadn't heard from Molly in three weeks but the memory
tapes were replaying in the waiting room. Kate turned on the
radio in her studio hoping for something diversionary to sing
along with. After flipping the dials back and forth without suc-
cess she returned to her table and tore the drawing in half. Then
she held both pieces next to each other as though they followed
in sequence instead of being two components of the same movement. It was a simple pencil sketch of a woman's face. She had
seen the woman come out of the movie theater that afternoon,
when Kate stood across the street watching Molly tear tickets.
This woman had huge lips. She decorated them with a metallic
pink like the Formica in Los Angeles kitchens. She had eyes the
shape of olives and straight black hair. By taking her depiction
of those lips and placing them next to, instead of underneath,
the eyes, Kate was forced to confront the mouth first, to make a
relationship with it before discovering those oil-cured black
things. The order changed the effect because, after seeing the

obscenity in that mouth, one experienced a monstrously seductive face. Then the greasy eyes came as a quiet surprise. The viewer learned from this sequence that the mouth was actually all that the face had to offer. If it was viewed at once in its entirety, there would have been no expectation. No movement.

As she stood across the street from Molly, sketching, Kate had wondered *Does she see me?*

When Kate had stopped designing for theater years before and started designing for herself, it was because she had gotten tired of decorating. She only wanted to confront directly. She needed more control. Her final stage production had been Genet's *The Blacks* in the early seventies. After the run she and Peter had gone away to the sea for one quietly spent week. There, Kate wore his sweater and sat in the evenings on a porch overlooking the water. She would read, draw, sip brandy.

"I can't stand actors," she'd said, suddenly, surprised it had come out so definitively.

"That's because we're different," Peter had answered, absorbed in his work.

"Who? You and me?"

"No, Katie. You and me on one hand and actors on the other. You and I go quietly into rooms, close the doors and, once all alone, begin to work. When we finish there is something that exists apart from us, whether a solid object or an event. But we walk away from it while others are having the experience. While they're watching we can be off making something new or drinking ourselves to death, as we like. Actors need the approval in their faces."

"Well, I'm tired of them," she had said, looking at Peter as he worked on plans. His sunburnt brow was furrowed in concentration. His skin was too fair for the sun. No matter how much he protected himself, it always burned. She had always watched him work to a secret internal rhythm, much the same way people now danced silently down the street wearing Walkmans. You knew they were hearing something you didn't hear. But it was hard to know exactly what.

"I'm leaving the theater," she told him then as the sea began to slide into the sunset.

Peter looked up and laughed easily like he was entertained.

Kate saw him thinking, *She's so cute*. Kate recognized that look. She'd used it with her own mother whenever she felt generous. It said, *You don't understand but I'll let it pass*.

Now, years later in her studio Kate looked at herself in the mirror. She was aging but it was all in her face. She shifted the glass so she could see herself standing against the wall. She wore a man's sleeveless white undershirt and stood demurely holding her brushes.

Kate had never painted Molly. She spent a lot of time looking at her when they were together, but she didn't want to own a painting that couldn't be shared with Peter and couldn't put him through the ordeal of watching her work on it, watching her live with it. He would know how recently she and Molly had been together by how quickly the work progressed. But the first time she had seen Molly's vulva in the light she'd realized it was a color whose name she did not know. It was the meat of a green-gage plum, dusted. She had gone home to her studio that day and mixed it. Then she painted one side of her studio that color and ended up thinking of it as starlight. Normally she painted with her head turned away from the wall, but whenever she wanted to be in starlight Kate only had to look up.

The buzzer rang on her intercom. It rang once. If that were Molly downstairs coming to make up, she would have rung twice. That was their code in case Peter was in the room. Kate didn't answer. She looked at her bookshelf. On the top left-hand corner were all her books by Wilhelm Reich. She'd long ago outgrown his theories but still loved the titles. They all clearly evoked distinctive shapes. There were so many to choose from: *The Invasion of Compulsory Sex Morality* sounded like a midnight movie. *The Bioelectrical Investigation of Sexuality and Anxiety* could be a new album by Talking Heads. There was always *The Function of the Orgasm* but that should be saved for someone's autobiography. *Ether, God and Devil* was clearly an opera. *The Mass Psychology of Fascism* should be read by everybody. But then Kate settled upon the right choice, the right shape: *People in Trouble*.

There was a knock at the front door.

She looked through the peephole and saw a short black man.

"Who is it?" she said.

"Census," he said, smiling.

She opened the door but stood in front of it so they could have a conversation without him coming into her studio. She'd heard stories of strangers pushing in through the front door and always took precautions.

"Hello, I'm conducting a survey on tenant perceptions."

"What organization are you with?"

"I'm with the Tenant Survey Organization."

He took out a laminated identity card. Underneath his picture it said "Tenant Survey Organizer."

"Okay," Kate said, not wanting to be excessively paranoid.

"How many apartments are there in this building?"

"Twenty-two."

"How many families?"

"How do you define family?"

"How many single people?"

"I don't know," she said.

"How many blacks?"

"Three. Why are you asking?"

"How many homosexuals?"

He looked at her as though that question were perfectly standard.

"I don't know," she said, mostly because she didn't know how to count herself. "I've got to go now."

"Please, two more questions and it will be complete. I only get paid for a complete questionnaire."

"Okay."

"How many single men?"

"More than five but I really don't know."

"How many narcotics abusers?"

"I don't know. Boy, the census has really changed since I was a kid."

"So has New York City," he said smiling. "But you wouldn't know. You're from out of town."

"Okay, I've got to go," she said.

She closed the door again. Just then the intercom buzzed. Only this time it buzzed twice.

13

MOLLY

△△

Their reunion unfolded thusly. Each one made her stand and stated her case. Then they back-and-forthed it for a while. Then they embraced.

"I only have two primary emotions," Molly said. "Anger and sexual desire. Then I have two secondary emotions: fondness and poignancy."

"Which ones apply to me?"

"Kate, toward you I feel anger and sexual desire, fondness and poignancy."

They let themselves feel each other and transform in each other's bodies before fighting a little bit and then they relaxed. This was the transition from life into love.

They took off their clothes and rolled naked against each other on their feet and leaned on a wall the color of starlight. After various places on each other's bodies and a variety of temperatures Kate stopped because she felt it was time. Her habit of rhythm told her so.

"I want more," Molly said. "I get turned on by making love with you. Think of something really sexy for us to do right now."

"All right," Kate said, leading her to the wardrobe. "Pick out something for me to wear."

"You've got your own costume shop," Molly said looking at the rack of play clothes. There were fifties prom dresses, huge elephant-bell paisley pants like Cher used to wear. There was lime-green crinoline, scarlet silk, black taffeta.

"I am a hard-core junkie when it comes to tactile beauty," Kate said. "Do you want me to choose, Molly? What about this?"

She pulled out a purple skin-tight 1960s pantsuit that would go perfectly with white vinyl go-go boots.

"Is this an original?" Molly asked.

"Oh, yes," Kate answered. "I have a past I can't outrun. Before I met Peter I used to go to Max's Kansas City you know. So, do you want me to wear this?"

"No."

Then Kate unhooked a white leather miniskirt with a huge black vinyl belt.

"Mod?"

"No," Molly said. "Too *Life* magazine."

There were enough accessories to open up a branch of the Salvation Army. This was clearly the result of a lifetime of regular, systematic inspection of thrift stores, finding great things and then taking good care of them.

"How about this?"

It was a handmade black dress of solid lace, designed to blow like grillwork over a bare body. It would obviously look incredible over Kate's breasts.

"Yes."

There was music. There were pulled shades and candles, a simulated night for these late-afternoon lovers. Molly sat back in a cushioned chair and watched Kate, thinking she was so exciting to look at under any circumstances because no matter what she was doing she was always so many colors. Then she watched her dance.

At first Kate seemed nervous, self-conscious, not free within her body, but encouraged by Molly's absolute joy, she relaxed and gave her lover this pleasure more freely.

Molly leaned back against the bed, hearing the sounds of day coming from the street, but sitting in the artificial evening.

When a person dances for her lover, Molly thought, *she may want to dance sexy and close or just want to move. Both are great. Neither requires permission.*

That's when the phone rang.

The two women watched each other's eyes, very still as the machine picked it up and the message played. Then the voice came on. Kate went to the machine.

"Hello, Peter?"

She turned her back, not so much for privacy as for concentration. There was nowhere to go in the tiny studio, so Molly sat very quietly in the chair with her eyes closed. Kate was going to take her time and not alert Peter to any other consideration. It was to be a normal conversation. They talked details. All details. The contents of that day's *Times,* including which airlines had proposed merger. The plight of the American farmer. Something having to do with percentage points. Both Kate and Peter clearly believed in quoting statistics. Molly moved to the bed, it was so clean and soft.

I really should get organized enough to have clean and soft matching sheets, she thought. She looked through the books on Kate's shelf. Any distraction.

Thank God, Molly thought as Kate and Peter finally got to the op-ed page. *I'd so much rather be the lover sitting here in silence than the husband being lied to on the phone.*

When she hung up, Kate took off her dress and placed it carefully on a hanger. Then she came to lie next to Molly and held her breasts in her hands.

"What's this?" Kate said, finding an extra texture between Molly's legs.

"Take a look."

Molly watched Kate's face framed by Molly's legs, one cheek

against one thigh, looking at the layers of her cunt and realizing how specific they were.

When it became that time when Kate had to be accounted for they parted. Something about that close loving and sexy sharing disappeared for Molly as she put on her clothes. While Kate readied herself for the next event, Molly left something of herself behind, as anyone does who begins an experience with another person and always finishes it alone.

14

PETER

△△△

Peter examined himself in the window of Tiffany's. He was in no rush. There was plenty of time until he had to be at the theater by five. He could run uptown and down again by then and still have an hour to check up on things. He had to be constantly vigilant with technicians to ensure the designs were completed with perfect accuracy. Every instrument must be precisely focused or the lighting would have no soul. It would be muddy, not crisp. Sometimes muddy is the best choice, of course, but it must be chosen. Whenever he worked a show with dubious structure, like this one, he could correct the shape without anyone ever suspecting. When an actor crossed the stage for no reason, Peter could give him a light to step into, which was at least an illusion of meaning. That's what it was to build shape. Technicians were grunts for the most part. If they could be artists they would have been. So they didn't care as much as they should and often violated the design by being sloppy. Peter was never sloppy. He was diligent.

He continued down Fifth Avenue, stopping suddenly in front of something very unusual. There was a billboard, of all things, hanging over Rockefeller Center. It was Ronald Horne's huge nondescript face, about two stories' worth, and underneath his nostrils in red, white and blue, it said:

Horne: For a Better America

After that Peter walked for a minute and then decided to step into Saint Pat's. Peter often walked into churches but he never got down on his knees. He never lit a candle. He just sat back and watched the show. There were a lot of tourists in the cathedral on Sundays. They were not only Americans with mobs of towheaded kids fresh from hotel breakfasts, but also wealthy visitors from Latin America in good suits. There was a sprinkling of African students with Instamatic cameras dangling from their languid wrists. Asian families lined up for photographs in front of someone's patron saint. There were street people everywhere who just needed a rest, trying to be inconspicuous in the pews. In fact, it seemed that every time Peter entered a church, a park or waiting room anywhere in the city, there were street people looking very tired. Every square of public space was occupied by someone asking for money or too out of it to be asking. But in the cathedral they were seated right next to little-old-lady good Catholics in tiny hats and gloves with patent leather pocketbooks and legs that could easily snap. On the edges of the crowd were visiting nuns traveling in packs or in couples on vacation. Peter wasn't Catholic but he often ended up in Catholic churches. They were everywhere, like Sheraton hotels. You could go anywhere in the world and there they were. His father hadn't belonged to any church. His mother went when she had to. She'd dragged her son along enough times to be sure he knew everything he'd need to be able to participate. But Peter remained faithfully unaware of the larger meanings behind the rituals. The priest entered. They all rose. An organ played. There were murmurings in various languages and constant movement as people came and went from their pews. After all, this cathedral was a major tourist attraction. This wasn't some quiet neighborhood church.

Peter made wishes. He always made the same ones, in the same order. He had kept those wishes in that order for years and years. He wanted to do good work, have it be recognized and stay healthy. Kate should stay healthy too. These didn't seem to be outrageous demands. And he wanted to be loved. As he was reciting his own private liturgy, about forty men stood up together from among the worshipers and turned to face them. These forty men turned their backs to the pulpit while the service was in progress. Peter's eyes happened to focus on the face of one who seemed somewhat familiar. Perhaps he lived in the same neighborhood. The man was thin and unsure of what he was doing. He was lanky and older with a gray mustache and bushy gray hair. He was uncomfortable. The man wore a black T-shirt with a pink triangle and the word *Justice* across his chest. It did not make him look like Superman. He was an anxious, regular guy. All the men had the same shirts. Some were robust and effeminate. Some were shy. They were all strong-willed and very serious. The men stood with their backs to the priest who continued his service as though nothing was happening. One of them held up a sign that said Living with AIDS for Two Years and Five Months—No Time for Red Tape.

These are men with AIDS, Peter realized. *Forty of them. But that one doesn't look like he has it. He looks like he works out. The thin one has definitely got it.*

He took another look at the familiar one and decided that he had definitely seen him somewhere before and that that guy probably didn't have it.

That black man, thought Peter. *I wonder if he's gay or if he got it from drugs.*

Then the black man spoke.

"The church is the world's most powerful hypocrite," he said. Peter noted that the man's voice and gestures were campy.

They shouldn't have let him be the spokesman, Peter thought. *They should have picked somebody more masculine, so people would be more sympathetic.*

The man kept speaking.

"Why don't all you gay priests and nuns come out and get the church off the backs of your brothers and sisters? Stop spending poor people's money trying to take away everyone's sexuality. Spend it on affirmative care for people with AIDS."

The crowd behaved pretty well. All these months of media blitz had prepared them in some way for this moment. A flurry of simultaneous translation into a variety of languages subsided once the audience was fully informed as to the content of that man's speech. Some of the visitors murmured with disapproval, others with compassion. Some looked like they wished they hadn't brought their children. Some tourists brushed it off as one of those "typical New York experiences" they'd heard so much about, then prided themselves on actually encountering. Some took pictures with flash. The men stood quietly, the worshipers sat quietly and the only noise was the voice of the priest droning over the sound system as though these men were nothing, as though they were not there. Then the mass was over and the men filed out. Peter decided to be natural and went to the front steps trying not to express any opinion to anyone who might be looking at him. It was a windy day, suddenly, for the first time all season. Some of the men were cold because they had not thought to bring sweaters. They stood around not knowing what to do for the rest of the afternoon. The ones who were used to being sick always carried sweaters, which they put on over their T-shirts. Then they dispersed, quickly. Some went off to have coffee, others went home to rest. Once those shirts were covered, they stopped looking like gay men with AIDS. They looked just like everyone else.

That, thought Peter, *is their most effective trick.*

15

PETER

△△

The play he was designing that week was called *Crossing the Border*, about a love affair between a Mexican migrant worker and a Russian émigré nuclear physicist. It was a musical. Peter knew he couldn't work the best material all the time and that really his finest work was ahead of him. He'd always dreamed of designing for the greats, for Richard Foreman or Bob Wilson or the Wooster Group. But those jobs were sewn up by an elite clique. So in the meantime he had a generally accepting attitude about the work that did come his way.

Peter's new intern was waiting for him inside the theater. He had been working all day but was wearing a suit and tie. Every time he climbed up the ladder, the intern carefully took off his jacket, unbuttoned his sleeves, folded them twice up his forearm and then climbed. When he came down again he put his clothing back in order immediately. He was a short black man named Robert who had just graduated from Yale Drama School and was assigned to Peter by the playwright, who was an old college buddy of Robert's father. Something about him annoyed Peter deeply. He was organized, true, but he was businesslike, that was his problem. He looked like a stockbroker, not an artist. Robert carried a briefcase. He never opened it balanced on one knee. He always laid it down deliberately on a flat surface and snapped the metal clasps so that they clicked and popped at the same time. He had been one of five black students in his prep school and one of five black students in his program at Yale.

He moved similarly to Peter, like a man who knew he could have been in finance but chose something more dangerous and obscure. But his briefcase reflected those other options a bit too blatantly for Peter's tastes. Inside it were little compartments for tools and a tape measure. He had smaller cases to hold his brand-new stencils for drawing leikos and Fresnels. At Yale he had learned up-to-the-minute technology for the various applications of mechanized light.

"I supervised the put-in," he said. "And I programmed the cues."

"I hate computers," Peter said trying to be personal. "I've refused to learn how to use them. It is a lot more interesting to try to run a show by candle or flashlight than to push one button and have everything done by computer."

Robert sharpened his pencil.

"Okay," he said, meaning nothing. "Let's run the cues."

Then he carefully removed his jacket and draped it over the back of his chair, folding his sleeves up his brown forearms. He had clearly been one of those kids who wore suits to school. A kid who was most comfortable in a jacket.

"Okay," Peter said. "The audience has come in and taken their seats. So, flick the houselights and then, take them down."

"They don't flick," Robert said. "They are not programmed to flick. They can go bright or dim, on or off, but not both."

Peter couldn't imagine what to say. He felt very tired suddenly. He felt older than he'd ever felt in his whole life. His role was becoming obsolete. He was being replaced by something with a level of information and ability that was not higher than his.

"Do you know how to make lights out of coffee cans?" he

asked, hearing himself creak like someone's backwoods grandfather asking "Do you know how to make a fishing pole?"

"No," Robert said.

"No," Peter repeated, completely unprepared.

"No," Robert said. "Why would I want to?"

That, Peter thought, *is the difference between theater and science.*

After the cues were run Peter did warm up a bit because Robert had done everything perfectly. He sat back and watched the young man roll down his sleeves.

"Do you know anyone with AIDS?" Peter asked, suddenly. For one second he panicked because maybe Robert had AIDS, but then he looked at him again and decided that Robert was not a homosexual. He was probably a virgin or else had the same girlfriend since high school on whom he made a lot of demands.

"Yes," he said. "Of course." Then he said, "Do you have AIDS? I'm not afraid of people with AIDS. I can still work with you if you have AIDS."

"No, I'm straight."

Peter watched Robert's facial muscles. Throughout this entire encounter he had not changed his expression. He would have stayed calm even if Peter had said yes, because Robert was growing up accustomed to being with dying people.

"My father's lover has AIDS. He was already in dementia when they gave him the AZT. He was walking around on a cane like an old, old man. The AZT brought him back. He has a lot of nausea and diarrhea but he's still there. You can talk to him and go places with him. He's an actor. He was around in the sixties."

"I used to work in black theater," Peter said, realizing immediately that the man in question might not be black, and then added, "In the sixties" to pretend that was the connection.

"I'm not interested in black theater," Robert said. "I don't care about a woman in a black leotard doing jazz monologues. I think black actors should be able to play any parts they want to play and not always have to play black."

"Well," said Peter, relaxing into his favorite kind of distance: discourse on the role of theater in everyday life. "Of course actors should be able to play a wide range of characters but community theater is an important training ground."

"You don't know anything about black people," Robert said with the same tone he had used to say, "Do you have AIDS?" "Do you know what kind of music young black people listen to? They don't listen to jazz and they don't listen to blues. They don't listen to soul or R&B. Did you know that? Have you been keeping up to date?"

"No," said Peter, "I'm out of date."

"You should correct that," Robert said. "So that you at least know what it is you feel superior to."

"I'm totally out of date," Peter said. "I have no idea what's going on."

"Look," Robert said, swinging his jacket over his shoulder and letting it hang from one finger like the guys in the ads for Harvey's Bristol Cream. "Just watch two hours of TV a week and you can find out."

He snapped the two metal clasps on his briefcase, swung it by the handle off the table and smiled at Peter as though he was the oldest man in the world. As though he, Robert, was in charge now.

"I want to get a job on the new Horne musical opening on Broadway, *Ronald's Dream*. They've got lasers. Do you know anyone there?"

"No."

"Or Stephen Sondheim. Do you know him?"

"We were at the same party once."

"Well then."

Peter watched the boy walk out the door. Then he went into the house manager's office and took out the portable TV. He plugged it in and waited. There was a show on called *Lifestyles of the Rich and Famous*. Some guy went around interviewing movie stars in their luxurious homes and the audience watched them play tennis and cook. The most startling aspect of the lives of these celebrities was that they could be so famous and at the same time Peter had never heard of any of them or any of the shows or movies that they appeared in. Then Peter reached over and switched on the office radio, flipping through all the stations from Top Forty to country. He didn't know one song. He had never heard of any of the groups. He put his hand up flat against the right side of his face and thought for one fleeting second that he had turned into a very silly man. He flipped to the jazz station and listened to that for a while. Then he went home.

When Kate came back from the studio that night she asked what he'd done all day.

"I listened to jazz and worked on a show," he said. "Working on a show" was the perfect way to explain away any block of time. Then he raised his eyes to hers and saw that she had that look. She had on her sunglasses and her scarf and too much lipstick and a big smile with lots of "yeah"s so he knew that she also had a secret because she was being much too polite.

16
KATE

△△△

By the end of October Kate realized that she had developed a habit of taking the same walk once or twice a week down the same street. Only the weather changed. The neighborhood was still jumping, though, with people trying to have their last out-door party, their last street-corner conversation before the cold weather's isolation. There were so many people on the street asking for money.

During the many months of late-night walks home from Molly's Kate had often wondered, *Have there always been so many?*

There was a huge black market on Second Avenue every night after eleven between Saint Mark's Place and Seventh Street. You could buy anything. There were people selling hot ten-speed bikes for thirty dollars and hot three-speed bikes for fifteen. There were crates of brand-new tape recorders and cassettes and CDs with cellophane still around them. But there were also entire contents of various people's ripped-off homes that were pulled out and excreted onto the sidewalk. You could buy half-used tubes of oil paint, half-eaten jars of peanut butter, plants, worn bedroom slippers and dirty towels. There were endless answering machines with the messages still on them and endless leather jackets.

There was something very different happening when Kate walked alone than on all those late nights walking with Pete. Coming home from some event she'd walk with him and look at him and talk to him and not see much of anything else. But coming home alone from her lover's had changed all of that. Men now talked to her constantly because Peter wasn't there. They said anything to her that they liked. She stood out, of course, with that coloring, especially late nights smelling of sex. Instead of Peter's wide mass next to her like a wall or a shield, she was in a wind tunnel, completely alone and unguarded. Kate pulled her shawl around her chest. Coming back from Molly was the first nighttime ritual she had experienced without Peter standing next to her and it changed what she saw when she walked down the street.

Some nights she wanted to get home as quickly as possible because she was tired from making love and would have preferred to just stretch out to sleep on Molly's rough sheets. But she couldn't. Or, sometimes she got so turned on by making love that she wanted to do that for hours, but she couldn't. Peter would be so hurt. So, she stumbled home instead and silently slipped into bed. Or, she'd get turned on on the walk home, thinking about what she had done and would make love with Peter when she got there.

Having a girlfriend makes sex better with your man, she thought.

Or, sometimes, if he was awake, they'd sit up at the kitchen table over a beer or tea and she'd make up something that had happened at the studio. Something very rich and specific. Or she'd get home and he'd still be at work, so she'd regret having left Molly so soon, or revel in a moment to herself or feel lonely for Peter and wish he'd get home. But some nights Kate went home very slowly because she was swimming in sex and felt some special power and explanation for watching things more closely. You see so much more when you walk down the street alone. That's why people work so hard to avoid walking alone too often. What people see when they're alone can drive them mad.

The first time Kate and Molly had made love was easy because Kate had decided not to decide anything. She did not consider even one consequence.

"I love your breasts," she had said, lifting them in her hands, letting them fall over her face and squeezing them together so she could suck both nipples at once. "I love your caramel eyes and your mustache and your breasts and your buttocks and your clit."

She was lying back in Molly's arms feeling nervous and open and silly, being held by a woman that way. Even though Kate was long, she was also very light and could be carried through the making of love.

"What animal are you?" asked Molly. "You're sleek like a mink but the size of a panther. Only it is the color that dominates everything. To give you a coat of black fur would be a lie. Is there a red fox who is like a swan but warm, that growls, who can turn into a tree to be watched and only then decide to bend? What do I have in my arms tonight?"

"Let me smell your breath," Kate said. "Mmmm, so sweet."

"That's because I've been eating you for the last half hour. Do you know why I like eating you? Because I like your come all over my face."

"No wonder men like big breasts," she said. "Who wouldn't? This is my favorite part."

She slid her hand back and forth over the slope in Molly's waist. "This shape, what is it? How can you say what this is, this hidden incline?"

"It's just because I'm female."

"Men are getting more female," Kate said then, becoming chatty and thoughtful, like she had just put on her eyeglasses. "At least in New York City."

That was over a year ago, Kate thought now, pushing her hands into her pockets and pulling the shawl more tightly around her shoulders. *I would never say that now, knowing the way she hates men. Imagine me having brought up men at a time like that. Shows how deeply I care for Pete, I guess, he's always on my mind.*

Only certain kinds of people are out alone with regularity late at night. Some are going somewhere and the rest are already there. That particular night four people stopped and asked Kate for money. And because she needed something to identify with this transitional state between Molly and Peter, she took a moment, on each occasion, to pull out her wallet and offer them something. The exception was a white wino sitting on a stoop who was too fucked up to stand and receive it. He expected her to come over and deliver, which was something she was not prepared to do. Especially since it would go directly to alcohol and not a more acceptable vice like food. But she did give to a disoriented black man wearing too many coats. He held out a paper cup and mumbled without acknowledging her gift. In fact, he didn't see her at all.

There were so many people living on the street it was unbelievable. Surely there were more now than there had ever been. Kate was warm and wet between her legs. She brought her hands to her face for Molly's smell, which was still on her fingers.

"Do you have any extra change?" a tired woman in gray clothing asked. Actually, it was her skin that was gray, her clothes were nondescript. "Thank you for stopping," she said slowly, articulating. "And God bless you. It is people like you who keep me employed. This is the one job I will never be fired from."

Do they say the same thing to each person, thirty times an hour, twelve times a day? Why aren't they rioting? Why are they standing so politely on street corners?

Kate passed graffiti on a wall that said Arm the Homeless.

She shook. If the homeless were armed, people like her and Peter would be killed immediately. They would slash the throats of everyone who had a nice place to live and gave only fifty cents.

Where do they go when it gets so cold?

"You don't ever go with men, do you?" Kate had asked that first night.

"I'm just not that interested in men."

Of course, Kate thought, *Molly was quite politic to answer so hesitantly.*

"They usually don't have anything to say about the things I'm interested in, so we end up talking about what they're interested in and I get bored."

They had been on a mattress on a floor surrounded by candles and dried flowers. There was that sweet smell of sex and the taste of the same on each of their faces.

"I'm going to take you to Ibiza," Kate said. Then she said, "Someone should dress you in red silk with one of those long slashes to show off your girlish back."

Five months later she had watched Molly wish on a star.

"What did you wish for?"

"A trip to Ibiza."

That's when Kate realized that Molly was waiting for her to make it come true.

"I remember words," Molly told her. "So be careful what you say to me. I waited for months for you to produce a red dress, or at least suggest going to the stores and trying one on. I tried on some myself but I never knew if it was the right one."

What could I possibly have said to that? Kate thought, feeling annoyed. Feeling slightly sorry and a bit put-upon. Molly was describing someone that Kate would never become. She would never pay that much attention, and that was fine. Peter didn't want that kind of attention.

Some day she's going to get so angry, she's going to slap me across the face.

Kate felt slightly guilty then, a bit uncomfortable. Her underarms hurt.

"You're easy to be with," Molly had said that first time, lifting Kate's body to hers so that their brown and red pubic hair met like an advertisement for National Brotherhood Week.

"What time is it?"

"One o'clock. I guess it's time for you to go."

"This was more comfortable than I expected," Kate had told her. "I wish I could stay the whole night. I really do. But I can't. Peter would be too hurt. Are you angry?"

"No."

Kate didn't know what else to say. She got dressed while Molly sat there, naked, watching her. That became a ritual between them. Kate kept her eyes on Molly's eyes until her own breasts and genitals were covered, then she'd switch her gaze to the door.

"Red silk," she had said, walking out the door. "Your back is so white."

Kate got to the front of her apartment building and looked up. The light was out. Peter was asleep. She felt filled with energy then. She wanted to run everywhere. She didn't want to go upstairs and lie still in a black house. On impulse she turned sharply and almost bolted toward her studio. Then she regretted the decision. Then she accepted it and started walking.

Now he'll think I've finally stayed out all night with her and won't believe me when I say I've been working. But it will be completely true.

This was such a complicated game of truth or dare. Peter forced her to lie to him in some ways and made her tell the truth in others. There were ways he wanted to be lied to, like about how much the two women saw each other and how important it had all become. But he wanted the truth when it came to the fact of Molly's existence. He wanted to hear about a meaningless affair with an unknown woman. Funny at first, the fact that it was a woman threw them both off guard. She didn't panic and neither did he, because they didn't expect that to mean anything. It just snuck up on both of them. If it had been a man it never would have gotten this far. Neither Pete nor Kate would have let it happen. Now Peter wanted to know everything and never see any of it. Kate was left with the responsibility of finding some acrobatic technique for accomplishing this unspoken request.

The first night Kate and Molly spent together, she'd walked home wondering, seriously, how Peter could have possibly committed himself to a lifetime of making love to a woman with such small breasts. The next time she and Pete had sex she was bursting with curiosity about this and many other questions pertaining to a man's view. She had rubbed her nipples in his face, like

Molly had done for her. She did it with a shake of her shoulders that she had never used before.

"Hey, you're in a good mood," he'd said. He was clearly surprised that she should be so sexy when it was just a regular night, when he wasn't expecting to make love at all.

But Kate got scared all of a sudden because something brand-new was making itself known. She saw right then that she and Peter knew each other so well sexually that if either of them was to introduce a new idea or act or word or response or fantasy or direction, sexually or otherwise, it would be so disruptive as to be obvious, because these feelings had to come from somewhere. Either she had to tell him the truth or blame it on the movies.

So, she had said it right away, that first night. She said that she had a lover and it was a woman whose name was Molly and she was younger. It would be half a year before Molly claimed he knew what she looked like. But that first night Kate told him that she loved him. That she would grow old and die with him. That he was her best friend and her best lover and nothing was as important or exciting to her in the world as he. Since then she had been losing sleep and walking home in the cold and heat and not having enough time for herself trying to keep all of that true. But it was those statements alone that ultimately convinced him to accept this preposterous situation.

17

MOLLY

△△

Another friend of Molly's died.

"That's the problem with having friends," she said. "You have to watch them suffer and die."

Jeffrey Rechtschaffen 1960–1988. She was in a great rage. She was so angry, clicking her jaw, uttering a variety of obscenities. She spoke them with such a fury that a crease appeared between her eyes in the morning and by that afternoon it was deeply embedded. She didn't know what day it was. She didn't look both ways crossing the street. She didn't think to button her jacket against the December wind. All she knew was anger. She alternately burned and tightened on the way to the bus station to pick up Pearl, who had come down for the funeral. Thank God for Pearl. Pearl let her know she belonged to someone.

She couldn't call Kate because they had just seen each other and she was supposed to wait for Kate to call her. More accurately Molly just couldn't face "There's someone here, I can't talk," one more time. Her head began to ache. She saw other people noticing her acting peculiar, so she tried to think of something else, something calming. But there was nothing else. It wasn't like turning to another channel on the TV because AIDS was on all of them, but only in the most idiotic terms. Everyone on television who died of AIDS got it from a blood transfusion. Or else it was a beautiful young white male professional with "everything to live for," and even then the show focused on his parents and not him.

Why can't they just say it? Why can't they just say "ass-fucking" on Channel Four?

Jeffrey had been a journalist for a gay newspaper in Washington, D.C. He knew every politician on Capitol Hill who was sucking cock. When a senator died of a "blood transfusion" Jeffrey knew he had been living with his boyfriend for years.

"That's how they do it," he said. "They keep the wife and five kids back in the house in Shaker Heights and the boyfriend's in the townhouse in Georgetown."

When Jeffrey was first diagnosed he decided to move back to New York City and worked at the AIDS Hotline whenever he felt well enough. Sometimes Molly would meet him for lunch right near the office. He ate strictly macrobiotic. Jeffrey had looked around carefully at treatments and he chose the creative visualization approach combined with various medications. He wore crystals. He carried a teddy bear and went for daily massage. He did yoga and said "I love you" to himself in the mirror every morning and night. It kept him alive for four years and three weeks when he was supposed to die in eighteen months. He hung on long enough to be wheeled in a wheelchair at the front of the Gay March on Washington so he could see what six hundred thousand homosexuals looked like smiling and cheering in front of the White House. He wore a shirt that said I Have AIDS—Hug Me.

Jeffrey said that the reason he lived so much longer than he was supposed to was that at the same time he embraced life, he accepted death. "Otherwise you die angry and the angry die quicker." But toward the end he changed his mind about that and got really furious. He said that the release would help him live longer. Molly thought that probably meant that feeling whatever he was feeling at any given moment meant better health generally.

The day he died the *New York Post* reported a bank robbery in midtown by two men in black T-shirts with pink triangles on them over which was scrawled *Justice*. They did not wear masks. They had no guns. According to Cordelia Williams, a teller interviewed by the *Post*, they slipped her a note that said "We have AIDS. We have nothing to lose. This money will go to sick people who have no health insurance." She gave them fifteen thousand dollars without setting off the alarm.

"My brother died of AIDS," she told reporters as she was led away in handcuffs. "So why should I send the police after those poor brave men?"

"You know what's really incredible?" Jeffrey had said over one of those macrobiotic lunches of steamed brown rice, steamed tofu, steamed adzuki beans and hijiki with mushroom and onions. "It is amazing for me to see firsthand the extent to which people calling the hotline will go to deny their homosexuality. There are so many closet cases out there, even when it is anonymous to a stranger over the phone."

Jeffrey was a long-legged Jewish gay man with a mustache; a cultural stereotype. He was always reading three books at one time like Walter Benjamin, *The Tao of Physics* and *I Once Had a Master*.

"Today this guy calls with pure macho panic in his voice. He thinks he has AIDS because he had sex once, two years ago, with a prostitute and he didn't use a condom. So I told him he had nothing to worry about. 'You probably can't get AIDS from women,' I told him. 'Unless you swallow their menstrual blood. Did you swallow her menstrual blood?' I knew he hadn't, of course. Too macho. So he says, 'But they say on TV you can get it from prostitutes. They said it on the movie of the week.' 'Don't believe what you see on TV,' I tell him. And then I try to explain to the guy the amount of men claiming to have gotten AIDS from women is so minute that they are probably just guys who don't want to admit they've been getting fucked in the ass or shooting drugs, so they say they got it from prostitutes. I told him it was probably impossible and a lot of people think that as far as sex goes, AIDS requires multiple exposures, so he probably didn't have anything to worry about at all."

Jeffrey's hair had gotten very thin. He sipped boncha tea. His clothes were all too big on him.

"But the guy wouldn't get off the phone. He kept hemming and hawing saying, 'Are you sure? Are you sure?' So I finally got the message and gave him what he wanted. 'Are you having sex with men?' I asked. 'No, no, no not me,' he says. 'Are you sure?' I say. 'Are you sure you didn't do it just once? Just to see what it was like? Once because you were really horny? Once because you were so drunk you didn't realize what you were doing and before you realized it, some faggot . . .' 'You know,' he says. 'Something is coming back to me now that you mention it. Yeah, I think I was really plastered. Totally smashed.' Like that."

Jeffrey sighed and ordered a piece of orange tofu pie.

"You have to give them every excuse in the world so they can tell you what they did without admitting to being gay. I think we should change the name of this country to the United States of Denial. This epidemic will never be taken care of properly until people can be honest about sex. Not even what they desire, just what they do. And you know, Molly, the world will have to stand on its head before the people who live in it will be honest about what they feel sexually."

Jeffrey's apartment was covered with fresh cut flowers and he always played soothing music. Even when he went into the hospital for the last time, his buddy from Gay Men's Health Crisis dragged along Jeff's cassette player, so he could go out listening to gamelan music. Gamelan and fresh flowers. But at the end, of course, being human, he panicked. He got mad at his buddy when Jeffrey was moved to intensive care. Then he refused to sign the release form saying he didn't need to be kept on life supports.

"I won't need it," he said.

Three days before he died Jeffrey got a letter from some people in San Francisco who were doing an anthology of journalists with AIDS. Did he want to submit a piece?

"No," he said, emaciated. "It wouldn't be fair. I mean, I'll be the only one in the whole book who is still alive and for the rest of my career I'll have to shake the stigma, you know, the AIDS thing."

18

MOLLY

▵▵

"Molly, do you realize how easily that could have been me?" Pearl said first thing after getting off the Greyhound bus.

"I know, I thought of that too. If women could pass it on as easily as men it would be us and our lovers that the world was mourning or ignoring. Instead it's just our closest friends."

Then they touched.

"I had a hard time with Jeff for a couple of years," Pearl said on the way back downtown. "When we would go out he was always looking around. I mean I'm glad I saw those days of disco, crystal, MDA, you know, 'I've gotta have it I've got to have more.' But sometimes I couldn't have a conversation with him walking down the street because he was always looking around at men and not listening or responding. I remember when the Saint wouldn't let women in. It was gross. But when AIDS happened men needed more friends. The back rooms got shut down and the bars needed more cash and started going coed.

Now it's easier to be close, but I always keep an eye on their body weight."

Pearl was one of those big, powerfully beautiful women who had to dress down to keep the men away. Molly felt about her the way people are supposed to feel about their families—someone to borrow money from if you need an operation.

"Boy, I'm glad I don't still live here. The city looks awful."

"I still like it."

"You're too loyal," Pearl said.

"Well, it's never boring. We had to go on rent strike because of Frankie in apartment twenty. The fucked-up guy with the weird leg."

"The one who got shell-shocked in World War Two and lived with his mother?"

"Yeah, Pearl, that's him. So he asked a neighbor to help him fill out his disability form and she found out that he lives on three hundred dollars a month, paying one hundred and fifty for rent. He can't afford electricity and eats all his meals at the Ukrainian Senior Center where dinner is a dollar. Then he tells her that after his mother died the landlord told him to move because his name's not on the lease. So, we went on rent strike and when we won he bought the building two six-packs of Budweiser. That's eight dinners at the Senior Center. Then this other thing happened with my bicycle. Did I tell you already? Why are you laughing?"

"No, you didn't tell me already," Pearl said, smiling. "This is exactly what I want to hear. Tell me about the bicycle."

"Well, Pearl, every day I lock my bike under the stairs. Then one day the tires were slashed. I excused it because the bike had been purchased hot for twenty dollars so naturally I had to expect a degree of bad karma."

"Naturally."

"But I was sure that the initial slashing would neutralize it. So, I replaced them and they were slashed again."

"Naturally."

"So I posted a sign in the lobby of the building saying, 'This Is Our Home. It Should Not Be a Place Where Bicycles Get Slashed.' And my tires got slashed again."

"I have to say I'm not surprised." Pearl's nose was red from the December cold.

"But I wouldn't give in," Molly continued, "to the idea that someone could continually slash my tires forever, so over and over again I replaced them."

"Molly, you never change," Pearl said. "You never ever change. You never give up. I know no one as desiring as you. So, you spent your paycheck on someone else's destruction fetish because you won't carry the bike up a few flights of stairs to the safety of your apartment."

"Look, I know it's a symbol of something inside me that has wrong and neurotic instincts, but I could not accept that my home was a place where a person could not park their bicycle."

"And what did Kate say about all of this?"

"I didn't tell her," Molly said, trying not to look too sheepish, but finally giving in to some kind of embarrassment. "It's too symbolic."

"You're still being hurt by this, aren't you?"

"Yeah."

"Molly, listen to me. I'm your best friend and I've been watching you going down over this married woman for too long." They were having one of those intense conversations that New Yorkers carry on in public places and still have privacy because everyone around them has heard it all before.

"Molly, you are a dyke. You do hear me? You have always been a dyke. You have never been that straight couple in the movie theater. Realistically, how are you ever going to pull it off with a straight woman?"

"But I love her."

"So, you can love someone else who's not going to make you feel like a freak. Get a lover who likes being gay and you'll be a lot happier."

"What is this, *West Side Story*? I feel like you're telling me not to date one of the Sharks. She loves me."

"I'm sure that's true."

They started walking again but had to wait at a traffic light while an animal rights demonstration passed by. There seemed to be a thousand people in vinyl shoes yelling in thick New York accents "Fur is murdah! Fur is murdah!"

"So," Pearl said, much more softly, "what about the tire cutter?"

"Oh yeah." Molly woke up, getting back in step. "Yeah, so everyone in the building began to talk about the slasher. Tony, the black guy on the fifth floor, the old one, asked if I'd caught him yet. The yuppie in number ten who is paying fifteen hundred a month asked if I'd called the police. Ralph, the junkie in apartment eight, asked if I had any suspects. Maritza, the super, asked why in the hell I didn't move my bike. And Kyle, the asshole in apartment one, asked me who I thought had done it. So, I decided that the people who had wondered if I had any suspects *were* suspects."

"Why?"

"This is New York City, why would anyone care that much unless they were guilty?"

"I follow your logic."

"So, Pearl, I told Ralph and Kyle that I had narrowed it down to the two of them and only they, therefore, knew which one really did it. Then the slashing stopped."

"What a step forward for strategic idealism." Pearl laughed.

"It is the triumph of good over evil," Molly said. "Isn't it? I guess that can happen every once in a while."

"Oh, Molly," Pearl said, "I'm so glad you're alive."

19

KATE

△△△

Kate took off all her clothes and stood in front of the mirror. She moved her head until she got the best angle: chin down, eyes wide, slightly angelic. Then she pulled the loose skin away from her eyes and opened the window. Her neck was getting veiny but it was either that or the beginnings of an extra thickness around the waist. She stood back from the glass and viewed her entire self. That body had become her pleasure dome, every act of it. She was doing something powerful. She was completing her sexuality. Her love for men was still intact but then there was this other set of relations.

Kate wandered around the studio touching her own objects. She tightened the glue, moved her charcoals over by the window. Kate gathered her sponges and dumped them into the sink. She washed her hands then, still naked, and picked up the magazine Molly had given her. She caught herself in the mirror again and then opened the magazine. Molly had handed it to her one late

△△

night after a guided tour of all the lesbian bars below Fourteenth Street.

"This is the Cubbyhole," Molly had said, starting with a loud, overpriced butcher-block place on Hudson Street. "It should be called the Glove Compartment. It mostly attracts graphic artists and luppies. That's lesbian yuppies in case you didn't know."

There was a video box there, where for fifty cents patrons could watch the video of their choice. She recognized some names, others weren't that familiar. They watched Madonna singing "Material Girl." Molly had called it a classic.

"Oh, Molly."

"What's the matter? You know what's weird about this place? It has too many fish tanks."

"Look," Kate said, pointing to the front door. "That woman, I know her. That's Susan Hoffman. Her husband is a sculptor. Susan! Hey Susan!"

"Kate, what are you doing here?"

"Just stopped in for a drink."

She could feel Molly standing next to her but Kate just didn't want to introduce them. She felt pressured.

"Me too."

"Isn't this strange," Kate said. "All these women dressed up like this. I mean, it's nice."

"Yeah," Susan said. "Nice."

Then Kate noticed that Susan was dressed up too.

"How's Dan?"

"Fine."

"Pete's fine too."

"That's good. Oh, there's my friend. See you later."

"Will I see you and Dan at Jack's party on Saturday night?"

"Yeah, we'll be there."

"So will me and Pete."

"See you then."

"See you."

Kate felt disoriented as she watched Susan negotiate her way across the bar.

"Isn't that great?" she said to Molly.

"Isn't what great?"

"That a straight woman like Susan can feel comfortable coming to a place like this."

"Why didn't you introduce me? By the way, she's not straight."

"Of course she is. I know her husband."

"She knows yours. Kate, look at the way she moves through the crowd. See how she touches the women as she moves past them and smiles sweetly. Watch. I'll bet you anything that's her girlfriend."

"Which one?"

"That femmy girl with the great earrings. See, wait, yep, watch that smooch. She came here to meet her lover."

Kate stared at the door for a minute and then drank down her four-dollar beer.

"But I know her husband."

"You think you're the only closeted married woman in New York City?"

"I am not closeted."

"Okay."

"How weird about Susan," Kate said. "It makes me feel like I don't really know her. Like I don't have any idea of who she is."

Molly didn't say a word.

"This is Kelly's," Molly told her, bringing them to a remodeled overpriced bar across Seventh Avenue. "It used to be exclusively for jocks. But since the renovation it got taken over by collegiate dyklings. Everyone here is femme."

"How can you tell who's femme?"

"That's the question of the year. After a while you just know. Usually it's the one who puts her arms around the other woman's shoulders when they're dancing."

"Which one of us is femme?"

"Neither. That's a joke. It's too early to tell because you still act straight. You have to be out a little longer before these subtle nuances take shape."

"Why are you always telling me what I'm going to become and what I'm going to think? How do you know?"

"You can bitch at me now, but later you'll see."

This time Kate kept silent.

"This is the Duchess," Molly said, dragging Kate in past the craggy-faced Israeli bouncer charging cover at the door.

"See how the windows are painted black?" Molly narrated. "It's nostalgia for the mud."

They had to pay a five-dollar cover, even though it was a Wednesday night and there were only three people in the whole place besides the bouncer.

"This dive is world-renowned for being overpriced and for having flooded bathrooms. There is usually some girl on black beauties breaking up with her girlfriend over the pay phone. It happens so often I used to think it was the same girl and they put her on salary for atmosphere."

"So what's next?" Kate asked, sincerely wondering.

They ended up at Tracks, a three-story gay entertainment emporium in the middle of nothing over by the river. At the front door was a sign clearly posted: This Is a Gay Bar for Gay People.

"It's gay-owned," Molly said. "Unlike some of those previous establishments. This is a chain. They have one in Washington, D.C. I think they have one somewhere else too, like Texas. It's kind of like a homosexual Howard Johnson's. But it has one thing in common with all those squeezeboxes and Mafia-owned dumps."

"What?"

"It's overpriced."

But it was inside that Kate found another difference.

"There are so many black women here," she said after ten minutes of fascinated silence. "And they're so incredibly dressed up. I would never think half these women were gay if I saw them walking down the street."

"Why not?"

"Well, they're just so elegant."

"Femme, you mean. You think the butches look gay and the femme ones don't."

"I still don't see which is which."

"It's like when people first looked at Impressionist paintings and they couldn't see the water lilies. You'll get used to it. Here's a shortcut. Which ones are you most attracted to?"

"That one," Kate said. "That woman is really beautiful. Look at her. Look at her mouth. And her, with the leather earrings.

Oh, look at that tall one with the long legs and red plaid kilt. She's gorgeous."

"Those are all butches."

"Even the one in the skirt?"

"Yep, now you know how to tell."

They danced for a while but mostly stood around.

"That woman over there," Kate said. "That woman is so beautiful I can't believe it."

"So, ask her to dance."

"I can't do that."

"Of course you can, Katie. This is a lesbian bar. That's why we're all here."

"Are you sure?"

"Yes!"

But at that minute a young strawberry blonde in a leather miniskirt and silky cream top came over and asked Molly to dance instead.

Kate watched them for a while, the way they picked up each other's rhythm and figured out how to move together. They figured it out rather quickly.

What do you know? she thought. *Molly dances hot with everyone. It's not just me. That's the way she dances.*

And for the first time ever, Kate felt jealous.

"Excuse me," she said, cutting in abruptly, "but I have to dance with my girlfriend." And took her to the floor, noticing immediately that Molly's arms went around her neck.

Then Molly announced one last stop.

"Where could we possibly be going now?"

"Shopping."

"At one thirty in the morning?"

"You know this city never sleeps. Anyway, it's a vintage gay porn store. You know that necessities stay open later than frivolous indulgences."

Kate felt one second of resistance before walking through the front door.

"It's fine in here," she said, without thinking.

"Excuse me?"

"I guess I might have been expecting sleazy old men jerking off into telephone booths."

Then she realized that she was surrounded by cocks. Mostly big ones. Mostly on beautiful young men. She started flipping through some of the magazines.

"This is how I know I'm not a lesbian," Kate said. "Because I'm turned on by cock. I like cock."

"All right, Kate," Molly said.

"I can't believe you're not."

"You can't be alive in the modern age and not associate sex with big dicks," Molly said.

"Well, I like it."

"Good for you. Does Peter have to hear you say, 'I like pussy'? Bet not."

"Well, I like cock." Kate said it again. She liked saying it. It made her sound dirty and polymorphously perverse.

"Have you ever said to Peter, 'I like pussy'?"

"No, I haven't," she said. "It has never occurred to me to say that. It wouldn't be appropriate."

Then she felt uncomfortable.

"Where's the women's stuff?" she asked.

"Ask the guy behind the counter."

The first thing that she noticed about the guy behind the counter was that he had Kaposi's lesions on his face. She knew that's what they were from pictures she had seen and some sideways glances at deteriorating men on the street, but never on the face of someone she had to interact with in an equal way. *How great*, she thought. *How great of this place to let him keep working like that.* Then she remembered that this was a gay place, so that particular brand of compassion could probably be expected. She wondered how many other people in the store had AIDS.

"Excuse me," she said, looking past the man's lesions to see his real face. "Where is the lesbian section?"

"Well," he said, smiling as if nothing was wrong, nothing at all. "Unfortunately most so-called lesbian porn is made by men for men but if you look over the really old material from the fifties and sixties there is some that's fun."

He came out from behind the counter and led her over to a solitary bin behind the videos.

"Here, for example, is a 1962 picture book disguised as a

socially conscious exposé. See, here is a classic black-and-white of two women eating each other."

He put it into her hand and walked away.

The caption said, "Lesbians are often better cunnilinguists than men."

That's true, she thought suddenly and was surprised.

When it was time to close up, Kate saw Molly making a huge effort to be in a good mood, since they only had an hour to get home and make love before Kate had to leave. On the way out Molly handed her a magazine she had bought and wrapped up in a paper bag, making her promise not to open it until she got home. That had been a week ago. She'd opened it a dozen times since then. It was a collection of transsexuals in various poses.

"I found this when you were looking at the muff-divers and thought of you immediately," Molly had said.

It was packed with photos of euphorically happy men in sexy, slimy, girly getups with hard pricks and big boobs. They looked so turned on. They turned her on with their dicks and tits, how excited they were.

Kate watched herself masturbate in front of the mirror. Her face showed great pleasure. She could rock down on her hips and swing into a low moan. She could dance around her studio being led by her own hand. When she masturbated against the white wall, her skin was so white that a voyeur would see no separation until the eyes. When she danced along the purple wall, the wall the color of greengage plums, she was a body tumbling over an ocean like the flying musicians of Chagall paintings. She masturbated. She could feel her orgone rushing inside her like a waterfall, like crowds of teenage girls held back from the Beatles, who, suddenly in a tearful frenzy, break free of the police and lose control. She was open in every way. There were no obstacles. She was streaming. Love streams.

20
MOLLY

△△

Pearl and Molly walked toward the church in Chelsea where so many men who had died of AIDS had their funerals. It was one of the first places to open their business to people with AIDS and their lovers. So it had become a safe environment for these most private of events.

The women were not talking about Jeffrey and they were not talking about AIDS. They had said everything they needed to say. All the rest would have been repetition because, after a point, there really was no way to resolve any of this. They had made love and cried and woken up together and lain about and eaten breakfast and talked about Jeffrey and gotten dressed.

Coming out the front door, Molly saw a short, husky black man waiting for her on the sidewalk. He was not leaning against the brick or sitting on the steps. He was jumping up and down instead, trying to keep warm.

"Molly, hey you got any checks for me?"

"Charlie, I took your name off my mailbox. This is my friend Pearl."

He shook Pearl's hand formally.

"Nice to know you." Then he said, "Molly, I got to talk to you for a minute."

"Okay, but only a minute. I have to go to a funeral."

The two of them went off together for a private conference by the mailbox, hands jammed in their pockets, feet stomping in various rhythms just to keep warm.

"Charlie, I gave up on you. We kept making appointments and you never showed up."

"I had things you know. I had to go see my mother."

"How's your mother?"

"Fine."

He kept looking around like someone who hated him could show up at any moment.

"Look, Molly, I need a certified letter for the Energy Assistance Program. This can mean two hundred and fifty dollars for me. I went to the shelter and it's crazy there. They keep the lights on all night and the crazies don't stop screaming. I need a letter that says I'm your roommate and I pay gas and electric so I can get energy assistance. The same kind you gave me before, certified."

"Okay," Molly said, "but I can't do it now. My friend died, I have to go to the funeral. I'll meet you here at nine in the morning and we'll get it notarized."

"Okay."

"Charlie?"

"Yeah."

"Show up, okay?"

He was gone very quickly.

Molly took out a pen and wrote his name back on the mailbox.

"Is he going to show up?" Pearl asked.

"No," Molly said. "Did you know that you have to have an address to get welfare? I didn't know that until this year."

Then they started out for the church.

"How's work?" Pearl asked.

"I go there and watch the movies. They change every day. My only problem is how to prolong my happiness."

"Oh, come off of it."

"Sometimes I get tired of having to choose between taking a subway or going for coffee, but I like being relaxed."

"Molly, you're going to have to do something substantial eventually."

"What do you suggest?"

"Uh . . . graduate school?"

"In what, computer science?"

"I don't know . . . social work? You already do it, might as well get a paycheck."

"Pearl, if I ever become a social worker, please shoot me and put me out of my misery. This is the Me Generation, remember? There are no more social services to administer. I'd have to wait until the return of the welfare state before there'd be any jobs to get rejected from."

"Can I ask you a personal question on a dangerous subject?"

"Sure."

"How could Kate have sex with her husband after having sex with you?"

"What is that, a compliment?"

Pearl took out a packet of Drum tobacco and started rolling a cigarette.

"Yes, I still smoke. No comments please. Anyway, I just brought up this tender topic because isn't that your beloved standing across the street?"

"Where?"

"Right there. You say she's not coming out, but take a look at that."

When Molly turned she stopped and they both stared through the traffic at Kate walking past Union Square Park. She didn't seem to see them at all. Her hair was orange against the green overcast cool and she was dressed as a man.

"Does she wear drag often?" Pearl asked with some doubt.

"Never, I've never seen that before."

"Well, something's going on."

Kate was a man. Anyone in the street would have thought

so. But she was a better man than most because she was so
strikingly handsome in her black suit. She strode powerful and
erect like a well-bred charming man. A male model perhaps. A
movie star. She didn't wear a white button-down. She was much
too stylish for that. Kate, the man, wore a soft blue shirt designed
for a sexy strong man's leisure. It was cut to hang from his neck
and muscles. Kate was thrilling. She was the most handsome
man on the street.

"Molly?" Pearl asked, not moving at all.

"What?"

"Do you fully understand what you're dealing with here?"

"No," Molly said, starting to walk again and then stopping
one more time to take a hard last look. "I have no idea."

21
MOLLY

△△

When a friend finally dies of AIDS there usually is not much surprise and often some kind of relief for everyone involved because the man they loved was suffering too much. Also, the people around him needed to go on. These funerals were frequent ghastly habits that crept into the structure of everyone's personal life. In fact, for Molly, at this point, there were a number of people that she only or mostly saw at funerals.

"Look," Pearl said. "There's Jeff's family from Rochester."

Huddled stiffly in a quiet corner were the out-of-place contingent of relatives experiencing a variety of emotions that ranged from pure loss to sheer embarrassment. They appeared to be as miserably uncomfortable with their surroundings as they were with one another.

Molly hadn't seen Bob Catmull since Ronnie's funeral but she had thought about him from time to time. He was a particular kind of personality that always reminded other people of something. He looked very healthy, she noted with relief as he smiled warmly, crossing the room.

"Bob," she said, reaching out. "It feels good to see you."

"Yes," he said slowly, being a tall sleek man with a mane of gray hair and a long tall Western drawl. "I am healthy and happy, praise God." It was half put-on, half deep cowboy roots. Bob had one of those voices heard over the radio in Nebraska advertising cattle feed. "I'm having some apartment troubles lately, but isn't everyone?"

There was something about the way he spoke that made the people talking with him want to sound that way too. So, after five minutes, there would be a room full of Brooklyn cowboys and one real McCoy.

"Someday," Pearl said, "there is going to be nothing in this city but condominiums and projects."

"Like *Clockwork Orange*," said Bob. "And we'll be the droogies, son of a bitch."

They all stopped talking for a while and looked around. Different people responded differently to funerals, and then again, it depended on who had died. Some people were usually numb. Some were resolved. Some had other things on their minds. Most cried their eyes out of their heads.

"Have you heard from Mario?" Molly asked.

"You know," Bob said, lowering his voice and then his head. He was about six foot four and had to bend way down to tell a secret. So, everyone around him always knew when he had something to hide. Also, since his head was higher than everybody else's, you could always see his expression.

"I just can't imagine another one of those times when you call up an old friend and get that damn tape announcing that his number has been disconnected. And I can't harbor the thought of writing to Mario just to get the letter returned, stamped 'deceased.' That happened to me last July and it was horrible. I have decided to wait until Mario gets in touch with me and I know and pray that he will."

"Look, Bob," Molly said. "Let's get together sometime. There are a lot of better places to meet than in church."

"I firmly agree."

They turned away from each other for a moment again and scanned, once again, the faces in the crowd just to see if Mario was there.

"Hey, Bob," she asked, pulling on his beaded belt, which came up to her chin. "Who is the guy standing over there in the corner?"

It was the same man she had seen handing out pamphlets at the vigil in early fall. And he was still just as femme. His brown skin shone against a pink wool suit, and she saw at least six rings through his left ear. He was involved in a serious, quiet discussion with three other men, one of whom was the surfer with the brown ponytail, who comfortably held the black man's hand.

"That's James Carroll. The hunk on his left is his lover Scott. They're very old friends. Do you know them? They're extraordinary. James in particular is a very clear and passionate man."

Bob said "passionate" with an emphasis on the p that brought out his Baptist roots and made him sound like the preacher man in a tiny white church in the middle of nothing but pasture.

"I got a flyer from him at the AIDS vigil. What's that group he's working with?"

"I'll tell you, Molly dear. There are not many choices right at the moment. If you are discreet you will know exactly what I am telling you now. There are a number of wonderful men who have absolutely nothing to lose. James is taking a sow's ear full of bitterness and transforming it into a silk purse."

The music started then as the gathering filed into the chapel.

Jeffrey had planned his own funeral and so it started with Nina Simone wanting to know what being free would feel like. The whole service was just like Jeff, sentimental, deliberate and goofy. There was a rainbow gay liberation flag draped over his coffin and fresh strawberries and figs for everyone to eat. There were silly pictures of him pasted up on the walls so people could walk around remembering this or that. Then different friends spoke about little things; his recipe for strudel, the time he dyed his hair blue, how badly he played the clarinet. They read aloud from some of his early newspaper articles against the closing of the baths. He'd said that if the city closed them, they wouldn't stop sex, just drive it farther underground and make it harder for the information to get out. There were many different feelings in the chapel listening to those words. They talked about the time he'd taken in a man who had no money and helped him to die, the time, the time. Jeffrey's was one short life filled with kindness and mistakes. He was another human being dead for no reason. A regular, special person. Then the tape played Billie Holiday singing "These Foolish Things," Molly thought, *they remind me of you, Jeff.* Then the family moved to the front and brought in a rabbi who got to stand up at the end and say, *"Yiskadol veh yiskadosh shemay rabah,"* which seemed to be the only part of the whole event that they could understand. That was when they cried.

Most of Jeffrey's friends wept here and there but generally got caught up in watching and listening to all that was being presented. There was no meditation time until the end when everyone walked out of the chapel into the yard to stand in a light flurry of snow. They held hands quietly and let the snow fall on their faces. It clung to some beards and a few long eyelashes and gave each person the chance to look up into swirling endless activity coming toward them with no visible beginnings. That's when Molly finally cried. Then that was that.

On the way out through the hallway onto the street Molly saw Bob again, this time conferring with James Carroll. They spoke to each other and both looked her way and smiled. She smiled back. They waved at her. She waved back. It was late afternoon by that time and the crowd was dispersing into the rest of their lives. But Molly stopped short on her way out and walked over to where the two men were standing.

"What was that all about?" Pearl asked as they walked down toward the West Village.

"He wants me to do him a favor."

"Who is he?"

"I'm not really sure. An old friend of Bob's? All I know is that he is the only person in the world who has come to me with something substantial to do in the face of all these funerals. I'm tired of feeling helpless in hospital rooms."

"What did he ask you to do?"

They both turned their collars up. They looked like two regular lesbians on a cold day. Only, Pearl looked very beautiful and Molly was only beautiful if you loved her. On every block there were men and women with no place to go who were bundled up under newspaper and old clothes or lying on ventilation grates to catch heat from the subway.

"He asked me if I would collect papers for him on Wednesday. He said that all I have to do is stay in the ticket booth at Cinema Village and men will come by to drop them off."

"What kind of papers? How double-oh-seven can you get?"

"I don't know, Pearl. Then he wants me to go over later that evening to an address he wrote down on this matchbook."

"To make the drop?"

Pearl had a *Twilight Zone–Untouchables* hush in her voice.

"Yeah."

"Where is it, Molly, some abandoned warehouse in Red Hook?"

Molly dug deep in her pocket.

"Jesus."

"What's the matter?"

"It's the same building as Kate's studio."

22
KATE

∆∆

Spiros had morbid taste when it came to choosing restaurants. In the last year they had lunched or dined at Exterminator Chili, Pasta Death and Saigon. This new place was called Embalming Fluid and was part of a chain of wine bars that Horne Realty had opened up around town. It wouldn't have been Kate's choice, but Spiros needed to have opinions on all trends in urban life.

He had already finished half a bottle of wine by the time Kate got to the restaurant. She knew it would take two more halves before any real negotiating could begin.

"How are you, my dear? My dear Kate, how are you?"

He was her dealer and so she had to trust him and absolutely could not afford to do so because after all, as Peter always pointed out, Spiros was not an artist. The most reassuring fact that she kept in her head at all times was that the only way he could make money was if she did too. Otherwise it was like being with Daddy again, intimate insecurity.

∆∆

Whatever contradictions were posed by Spiros, the old drunk who had made millions in the new country and stolen hundreds of thousands from the old one, he had changed her life. Opening up his world to her had brought Kate the necessary prestige and cash to live the way she wished. No more sets for bad plays. No more earnest art students. No more commercial design work. She had freedom from all this thanks to Spiros, the man who had taken more time with her work and career than anyone, even Peter. Spiros took the time to understand every detail because his income, in small part, depended on it.

They chatted. He had big lips. They began with the weather, glossed over Kate's suit and tie and moved on to more personal topics. That new artist. This old one. Two men had died. The Whitney Biennial. His daughter was going to Greece.

"Order whatever you want," he always told her.

It made life so much more pleasurable to have these occasional indulgences. Indulgence in this case being part investment, partly the reason for the investments.

Spiros was old and soft and white. He had soft hands and never behaved improperly with artists although he did have a habit of getting drunkenly overfamiliar with waitresses on occasion. His artists confided in him, as Kate did, because he changed their lives. How could she not tell him the truth?

"I spied on Molly from across the street, watching her going into a funeral. The mourners greeted each other very warmly. Peter was right, these are unusual funerals. There is a sincere but familiar grief, a practiced one."

"You don't mean to tell me that both you and Peter voyeur on AIDS funerals?"

"Yes, we're ambulance chasers."

"Well, Kate, that might make a good theme for a piece, you know."

"What a thought. No." She shuddered. "No. What disturbs me the most is Molly going off to another one of those funerals and not even calling to tell me about it, not letting me know in any way that she might need some extra love. She likes to stand next to monsters to prove to the world how good she is. She's good on purpose."

"Well, what other decent excuse is there?"

Spiros laid a pudgy hand on Kate's sleek one. Her fingers were longer and her fingernails were shorter.

"And Peter still sits there looking silly sometimes and older when he's tired. He speaks evenly, totally sure that he's right, will admit no doubts. We talk about new scripts, new lighting plans, what we saw at the theater, socks and our usual stylish conglomeration of interests."

She smiled.

"When we see friends he discusses Baudrillard and Jack DeJohnette and repeats his observations from night to night until he finds new ones."

"Those are fine topics for conversation," Spiros said gently.

"I know. We're both so tasteful and intellectual."

"However," Spiros said, watching the last drops empty into his glass. "As Thomas Mann said, 'Only beginners think that those who create, feel.' And to that I add *necessarily*."

Kate lifted her wineglass like a man.

Spiros watched her arm move. She saw him.

"Kate, I know what you are saying. You have the same opinions about a lot of old topics and struggle over the same issues and ask each other to run errands. Now tell me your new proposal."

Spiros sat back and watched her speak. Kate could see he was listening. She felt articulate and natural. She tried putting her hands in and out of her jacket pockets for emphasis and that worked well too. Then she discovered that straightening out her suit jacket occasionally contributed to her authority. In these clothes Kate felt capable of suggesting absolutely anything and making it sound reasonable. Then she was done.

"Kate. What you are suggesting is an installation. I am an art dealer. I only sell paintings that people can pay for with a check and take home in a cab."

Were her cheeks flushed? She had embarrassed herself. It wasn't worth trying to convince a gallery owner of something he couldn't make money from. Why had she been so naïve?

"But I do sense a new kind of seriousness in you, a new level of investigation and I want to support it as fully as I can.

Last week I was contacted by a prominent businessman, well actually his assistant for cultural affairs."

"What does he want, a mural in his medicine cabinet?"

"No, no, just the opposite, in fact. It turns out that the city, in preparations for upcoming mayoral elections, is about to make a token gesture to the arts. They have promised real-estate developers millions in tax rebates if they provide funding for public artwork on their properties. There are a number of projects under way to convert former public buildings, long in disrepair, into refurbished private space, relocating the public facilities onto barges. The mayor's office will be promoting and publicizing the efforts in a bus card campaign called 'Privacy Is Golden.' Now, I know that there are large areas of park and sidewalk space available that would be suitable for the piece you have in mind. I think I can help you get into this granting program. Frankly, it is your only available financial option and the work would be seen by people on the streets going to work, et cetera. It would not be shut up in some exclusive, out-of-the-way gallery."

She drank down her glass of wine.

"Interested?"

"Why do I feel suspicious, Spiros? I have never been involved with businessmen or corporations before."

"Well, your work is getting bigger now. It needs to be supported in a larger way. These men are the new patrons of our day. Better they should spend their discretionary income on the arts than on the Contras."

"But what if they spend it on both?"

"Look, Kate," he said, taking her hand again. "It won't be hidden away in their private offices. It will be seen by the people of New York City." He dropped the hand. "And that's the best I can do."

Kate thought she was going straight home from the restaurant but then decided on the studio but ended up back at the funeral instead. She stood across the street, watching what seemed to be the end of the service. There were Molly and Pearl in the front and a lot of gay men all around. *These people at the funeral* came into her mind like a sentence. The family stuck out. They looked miserable, crunched together shrinking from the community of mourning friends, not understanding any of it. They were denying themselves the comfort within arms' reach. They hadn't asked enough questions to be of use.

Kate's own parents had raised her to live comfortably. They had taught her to strive but differed on the goal. Kate still couldn't be real with her mother, even though she was past seventy. Her father had gotten quieter and quieter and finally died. Peter would be the same way. She thought of them all with great love.

She had vague memories of shapes that felt more like incidents than relationships. Something forbidden had happened with another girl. What was it? Her cousin had pubic hair, thick, black and slippery. It was secret and sexy to be excited by hair on your older cousin at the age of seven. Did she really want all this information? There were many more details, Kate was sure, but toward what conclusion?

She walked in the door of her studio. That family. They didn't find out who their son was, so when he died they couldn't understand his funeral. They couldn't find solace with his friends who had stood united before them. There was a deprivation that accompanies this kind of ignorance. She couldn't get them out of her mind.

23

PETER

∆∆∆

"What's this?" Peter said pulling at her necktie. "Is the Annie Hall look coming back?"

She didn't answer.

"How's the new piece coming?"

"I started out using a lot of earth colors, but then it got too purple, man-made colors and metallics, so I've moved away from that for a while."

"Still using the cutouts? I want to come over and take a look soon."

"Yeah, I've got the photos and some collage, using a lot of underpainting and then missing it and madly scraping with a razor blade."

Peter was looking for a way to make her laugh. Things had been so strained between them lately. He knew that she was seeing that girl again, but this time Kate acted strange. It was becoming hard to overlook.

"I'm going out for a walk."

She didn't say anything. Not "Can I come?" and not "Where are you going?"

We still have sex, he thought. *So what's the problem? Is Kate old enough for menopause?*

"Peter?"

"Uh-huh?"

"I'm having dreams in the middle of the day."

Finally, he thought with relief.

Peter went and sat down behind Kate on the couch. They liked to sit that way together, where he stretched out behind her and became just another cushion to sink back into.

"Human furniture," she said with a sigh of relief. This is what she always said when he did that for her. They could be normal. He could comfort her now as always. Nothing was going to change that.

"In my last dream I was going to Vietnam as a tourist. I forgot to bring my guidebook. I was sitting on the airplane, panicking. I thought, *This is what you get. How stupid worrying about a guidebook when people don't have enough to eat.* This wasn't war-torn Vietnam, this was the modern Communist one. *They don't care about your dollars here,* I told myself. *You fool, there are no tourist attractions in a people's republic.* Things we take for granted like airport signs translated into English are just details of capitalism. You know?"

This wasn't exactly what Peter had expected. He wanted something about fear, or her family. He wanted her to say, "Peter, I love you so much. I don't want anything to ever come between us."

He wanted something tender where he could be strong for her, not dreams about Ho Chi Minh City. She seemed older every time he looked at her. She was not staying in as good shape as he was. She wasn't sleeping enough and she wasn't working out. There was no way Kate could make it through the whole winter without getting sick.

"Are you eating enough, Katie? There's chicken in the fridge. Have you had any?"

"Yes," she lied. Then seemed to regret that. He reached over and touched her. He started to rub her neck.

"That feels good."

Everything was all right. He should watch himself and not let some lesbian make him paranoid.

"I'll take the garbage on the way out," he said. "I bought these new garbage bags because the other kind broke going down the stairs. Did the super fix the intercom yet?"

"No," Kate said. "Not yet."

"I talked to Don on the phone," he said, rubbing her shoulders. "He wanted to know what to wear to a job interview at the Public Theater. I told him to be clean."

"I would have said to dress exactly like Joe Papp, loose jacket, white shirt, no tie."

Peter started to relax.

"I got the tickets for tonight," he said. "It starts at nine. I couldn't decide between Pound's *Electra* or that Borges *Tango* thing. I figured the *Electra* would probably close first. Besides, we can definitely get weekend comps for the *Tango* but Carrie could only promise me weekday comps for the Pound. 'Seal sports in the spray.' Is that Pound?"

"I don't know."

"Of course you do. Let's look it up."

"I don't feel like playing that game right now," she said. Then she said, "I'm sorry, Peter, I'm not feeling that well at all."

"You always do that. You always say something really hurtful and then you apologize immediately after so that I can't get angry and you don't have to feel so guilty."

"I don't feel guilty."

"Well," he said, standing up abruptly and pulling on his jacket. "You should."

Then he waited for her to say something. He waited for her to say "You're right" or "You're wrong" or "Shut up," to engage him on some level. But she just closed her eyes and shifted away from his direction, curling into a napping position on the far end of the couch.

"I'll be back by seven," he said. "Do you want to eat before the show?"

"I'll have to see. I'm not really feeling very well."

△△ 103

"Not well like how?"

"Not that way. Just normal flu or something. Have a good walk. Bring me back some magazines."

For that art project, he thought. She voraciously clipped from magazines, anything—*True Detective, People, National Geographic, Personal Management, Heavy Metal.*

"Peter?"

"Yes?"

That's how they always were, calling each other back. Their hands were always in each other's pockets.

"If you hadn't had this life, what do you think you'd be doing now?"

"I'd be a dad," he said without any doubt. "Maybe teach school in New England. Make things in the basement after work. Coach Little League. Be an upstanding citizen."

"I could have been a housewife," she said. "An alcoholic one. Or a frigid professional. I probably would have been an art teacher in an elementary school having a twenty-year affair with the married science teacher, ignoring the janitor's advances and watching the legs of the twelve-year-old girls. What else do weird women do when they find themselves in normal places? I could have opened the Kathleen Connell Dance Academy on Main Street and put on *The Nutcracker Suite* every Christmas in the basement of the Calvary Church. I'd do my food shopping in a beige leotard and ballet slippers. Or, I could have been a whore at the Sly Fox Café in Covington, Kentucky. But with any of those possibilities I'd still end up going out in the middle of the night to buy my liquor and the only place open would be the mall."

24
PETER

△△

*Why did she have to say that part about the twelve-year-old
girls?*

Peter jammed his hands into his pockets as he walked down
Sixth Avenue. He knew she threw those things around just to
hurt him. She had to let him know she was going to do whatever
she wanted no matter how it made him feel. Fuck her. He could
have affairs too, he just didn't. There was that actress in *The
Blacks*, Sandra King. He could have had an affair with her. Her
skin tone was perfect for stage light. She had a smooth deep tan,
like fine leather. He hadn't lit many black casts before and he
couldn't stop looking at her in the light. Her hair was straightened, which was not the style in those days. She wore it back,
showing off a hairline that was a designer's dream, the way the
Mexican shoreline looks from an airplane. It framed her face
perfectly. Kate was still painting scenery then, and she often got
fed up easily and left early while Peter stayed working late. San-

dra had big bony features and her skin was pulled as tightly as her hair, stretched taut over her chest. She wore large earrings and jerked her hands up and down as she spoke, as though she were pulling herself up a bramble-covered hill. He wanted to see her by the ocean. He remembered a vivid fantasy of standing seaside on a cliff at night with his arms around her looking out over the water together until the first amber rays of dawn would sneak into the sky. So, one day, he slipped a cut of Bastard Amber into the gel frame and as she turned stage right, he brought up the blue and then eased in the BA slowly, maybe a twenty count. It was only up to level three but it was there and she was by the sea. Peter remembered how the night was cold but her body was warm and as the water growled onto the shore, he knew he'd be entering her and lying with her under many blankets.

In reality they did have coffee once. She was married to a Jewish actor. They had one child. She was worried about the usual things. After the show closed he didn't see or hear of her for years until one morning when they ran into each other jogging around Washington Square Park. She said she was divorced and working as a buyer for ladies' swimwear.

Peter was wearing a new black leather jacket. It was so soft and smelled great, like a comfortable chair or the country. It gave him some feeling of sensuality and security on those dark, cold New York City gray days. The winter made the streets quiet for a moment, almost reflective, and gave it the illusion of being safe and manageable. There were practically no loud noises at those times.

He stopped at the Cineplex Odeon Horne Quad Movie Center (formerly the Waverly Theater) to consider a movie. There was an action romance with hip young actors, a British import that was clearly slow, and two star vehicles. He could tell from the posters that the male star vehicle involved various forms of mechanized death and the female one contained a variety of fake foreign accents. Then he noticed two women, half his age, kissing against a car. He stared at them. They were beautiful really, both with long dark hair and he was glued to their absolute abandon, kissing so openly right there on the avenue. Their dungarees were rubbing against each other. One had her fingers hooked in the other one's belt loops. As the other kissed her neck she turned her head and then, accidentally really, her eyes met Peter's full on. She was flushed with cold and lust. As soon as she caught this man staring at her, she flashed a laugh like a knife. It was a weapon, a stare and an icy resistance. Her gaze was a powerful sexual defiance of him and his. But then their eyes locked in sudden recognition which transformed her expression. It literally fell off her face and clattered onto the sidewalk and was replaced, immediately, with guilt. It was so clear a change that Peter saw, in a jolt that froze his skin to the leather, that he had finally confronted Molly face to face and at the same time he had caught her cheating on his wife with another woman. He felt offended for Kate's honor and then ashamed for his own. But he had finally seen that face in full.

She has a mustache, he thought. *And she's fat. Not fat exactly, but definitely out of shape. Her clothes don't fit well.*

He was surprised. Kate took such care with how she looked, so he imagined that any woman she'd be involved with would too. A woman is a woman, after all. She should be attracted to the kind that she wants to be. But this one swaggered. He'd have known she was gay immediately. As soon as there was any real difference of opinion she'd be a real bitch, not conceding anything to a man, just for the principle. Then he'd have to make excuses to get away before she accused him of being a sexist. They were all like that.

Molly turned from him and spoke to her companion, who looked up at first but then turned away as well. They walked down the block holding hands and never looked back. Peter knew this because his eyes followed them all the way. Then he paid for the movie, not remembering which one he'd chosen, and headed directly for the men's room. Once inside, he stood in the stall sweating, holding his balls and rocking back and forth. It left a smell on his hands that he liked. His balls were leaking. Peter thought about the most unusual thing. He remembered a long-ago lost memory from college, of a day like this one in New England. John Craig stopped him in the school cafeteria to say that he knew a girl who would fuck five guys that night at her brother's apartment. Johnny would let Peter be one of those guys.

They all went over there and sat on the living room couch giggling at first and then somberly sipping Scotch as each, one after the other, passed behind the closed bedroom door. Fifteen minutes later, each would reemerge, tousled, flustered and grinning. Peter was last. He wasn't used to drinking and felt tingly and light. He was hard the whole hour waiting for his turn. But something about the smell of that bedroom made him dizzy when he first stepped in. It was rank, like a slaughterhouse, and there was scum all over the sheets. He took down his pants and she made a little wet cup on her stomach with her hands and saliva that he slid in and out of until he came. Then he stood up with his pants at his knees and looked at her and said, "Why are you doing this?"

But she just laughed. The expression on her face was so blank and frightening that he grabbed onto his balls and rocked back and forth, back and forth, holding on to a towline to safety.

25
MOLLY

Molly took Pearl to the bus station early Wednesday morning and spent the rest of it staring out the window over a cup of plain tea. At noon she wandered over to work, which began with a hello to Danny who ran the concession stand. They began every day by drinking Cokes with extra syrup so they could be peppy for the customers. She could eat as much as she wanted to of anything that couldn't be counted, which meant unlimited soda and popcorn but no Goobers or Raisinettes because they would show up missing on the inventory. Then she sat in her booth, put in new colored ticket rolls, filled out the cash sheet and did the crossword puzzle.

The double feature that day was *The Damned* and *The Night Porter*, so that attracted all the Nazi freaks and so-called decadent types plus a lot of masturbators and some film students. Every once in a while a thin nervous man would approach the window and not ask for a ticket. He would not reach for his wallet.

"Justice?" she'd ask, with the same inflection she used to say "Night Porter?" Then he'd slip a yellow piece of paper through the money slot and she'd say, "Thank you. Have a nice day."

Not all the men making drop-offs were that mysterious. A few sauntered by with friends.

"Wait a minute, will ya? I have to drop this off. Hi there. Are you from Justice?"

Then she'd smile and he'd smile and he'd go on his way. One guy got into the full spirit of things by saying "Thank you, sister," flashing a victory sign with two fingers on his right hand followed by a fisted salute. Either he was an old radical or he was showing off the manual technique he'd picked up at the Mineshaft.

All day long she collected little slips of yellow paper and never once looked at them, taking her assignment as a messenger quite literally. Then Kate came up to the window in fedora and pinstripe.

"Night Porter?"

"The Damned, please. I miss you. When can we get together? I'm horny. When do you get off work?"

Now that Kate was wearing men's clothes she'd gotten a lot more forward, Molly noted. And here she was coming and asking directly for things. Maybe it wouldn't take quite so many days for the phone to ring as it used to. On the other hand it bothered Molly a little to hear Kate say she was horny because that's what her husband was for and if he wasn't living up to the demands of his marital duties then why was this guy still in the picture?

"I have to go to a meeting tonight. It's in the same building as your studio. It has to do with AIDS. Do you know an older black man who lives there named James Carroll?"

"You know my hours are so weird that I don't get to see many of the other tenants, but I may have met him at some point."

"He's got a younger boyfriend, looks like a meditator."

"Maybe."

"Why don't you come with me? Why don't you sneak into this ticket booth for one moment and feel my ass while the boss is busy freebasing?"

Kate reappeared at quitting time and witnessed the final three drop-offs with great interest. She flipped through the papers as they walked along.

"These are all eviction notices," she said.

"I thought so."

"They're all from my new landlord."

"Who's that?"

"New York Realty. It's a Horne subsidiary, I think. See, it says right here that his company is the plaintiff . . . on every one of these cases. I just got the announcement two weeks ago that he had purchased my building, but I didn't get any eviction notice. Look, these three slips are all from my address."

"Do you know them?" Molly asked looking over Kate's arm. "There might even be more than these. I think there are three or four other people collecting today."

"Who are these tenants?" Kate asked, still thumbing through the yellow slips. "Pablo Guzman. That must be the Latin guy in apartment twelve with a diamond stud in his ear. And number five?"

"Isn't that the young guy with the punk haircut who wears sunglasses at night?"

"Maybe. And number three, O'Rourke. I've often wondered about him actually. He used to go out every evening quite late and come back three hours later. I could hear him locking and unlocking his door. Not recently though."

"I hope not. Cruising is no longer cool, I think. Who knows, actually. Anyway, it looks like all the gay men in your building are being evicted. Does it list the charges?"

"Pets. They're all being thrown out for having pets."

"Like dogs and cats?"

"Yes, it looks like every other gay man in the neighborhood is being evicted. How do they know who's who?"

"Well, we'll find out tonight," Molly said, moving in under Kate's arm. They kissed.

"Spare change?"

They stopped and both reached into their pockets.

"Hi, how are you?"

"Miserable. It's too cold. This is hard, very hard."

"Save the winos," said a wino.

They stopped and Molly gave him fifteen cents. Kate gave him twenty.

They waited at the corner for the light and kissed deeply. They passed a man going through a garbage can by tearing the plastic bags at the bottom and eating rancid food with his fingers. They passed a woman with a baby in a stroller. She was asking for change. Kate and Molly each gave her a dollar.

"Hey, Molly."

A black man in a woolen cap came across the street. He nodded quickly at Kate and then turned his body and spoke in such low tones that he brought Molly into a private conversation by making her stand closer.

"I'm sorry I missed you that time."

"I didn't wait too long. Are you all right?"

He looked awful. He looked fifteen years older.

"Give me ten bucks. I'll pay you back."

He smelled rotten. Molly felt sick being so close to him. He stank.

"Just ten."

She looked right into his bloodshot eyes the way all New Yorkers do when they're going to say no.

"Charlie, everyone needs ten bucks and you always need ten bucks and even I need ten bucks and I'm not going to give you money to go smoke coke. Do you want food?"

"Yeah."

"What do you want, pizza?" She was in a hurry.

"No, it hurts my stomach. How about some of that big bread French toast and eggs and some sausages?"

She reached into her pocket and felt around.

"I can't give you that much. How about eggs and potatoes and coffee?"

"Okay, over there though," he said pointing with his head to the sit-down coffee shop across the street. "That other one," he said, referring to the countertop place, "is terrible." His hands were too cold to take out of his pockets. "Food's just hot grease."

"Okay, wait a minute."

Molly ran across the street and leaned around the people defrosting over long bowls of thick soup.

"You see that guy over there in the red hat?" she said to a Polish waitress with no green card. "Let him order five dollars' worth of food and here's a dollar for you."

"Who's that?" Kate asked.

"He used to be my friend but now he's on the street. I can't let him in my house or he'll steal everything and never leave."

They kissed again and were stopped again. They each gave over the last of their change.

"Here we are trying to have a run-of-the-mill illicit lesbian love affair," Molly said. "And all around us people are dying and asking for money."

"It is absurd to see people suffering every day."

"And to be so untouched personally," Molly said. "That's the really scary part."

"What do you mean *untouched*? We see this constantly."

"Okay, Kate, but our city is so stratified that people can occupy the same physical space and never confront one another. New York is a death camp for thousands of people, but they don't have to be contained for us to avoid them. The same streets I have fun on are someone else's hell."

"Well, more and more artists are doing work about AIDS. There were shows at the Whitney, the New Museum, MOMA, DIA . . . more than I can list."

"So what does that do?"

"Molly, artwork is very political. It teaches people to see things in a new way. My artwork is my political work. Form is content. New forms are revolutionary."

"I don't think you would be satisfied with that explanation if it was happening to you."

"It could happen to me," Kate said. "It could happen to you."

"I'm not going to get AIDS," Molly said.

"Yeah, but you could be homeless. What if your building burned down or went co-op?"

"I would have to leave New York, I guess. But I am white and know how to read so I can always get a job, even a boring one. There will always be McDonald's."

"What if you get sick?" Kate said. "I'm sure you don't have any health insurance."

"I don't know," Molly said. "I have a lot of friends."

"What about when you're old?"

"Okay, you win. That's when I'm really going to be in trouble. I forgot your point."

"That it could be you or me, and if it was, my response would be the same. I'm an artist. That's political. Form is content."

"Okay." Molly was quiet.

Then Kate reached over and touched her, being conciliatory, now that Molly had given up.

"Molly?"

"Yeah?"

"I don't want to fight with you. I just want to kiss you."

When Kate put her arms around Molly on the street they became very obvious. They didn't disappear like she and Pearl did. They stood out. Anyone watching would have seen a peacock in a man's overcoat holding a significantly younger, more bewildered woman to her with some sense of passion.

"Let's check out the meeting," Molly said.

As they walked along the crowded sidewalk Molly could see that there were tiny jewels and particular human treasures in different spots along the way, but each one was surrounded by something very difficult and fearful. At the same time that Molly so clearly saw this decorating her path she also felt privately satisfied, having just been kissed and on her way to a destination. Her inside was safe, her outside was endangered. Why was she so protected?

"Why are we so protected?"

"I'm not protected," Kate said. "I'm a poor artist. I am not a powerful person in this society. Don't be so self-deprecating, it's unbearably righteous."

"You're not poor. Neither am I."

"Listen, Molly, when I was your age I was a lot more radical than you are, so don't lay that on me. That's your trip."

"Let's go to the meeting," Molly said. "Let's go there now."

26

KATE

△△△

James and Scott lived in two adjacent apartments on the ground floor of Kate's building. They had broken into the basement and built a large comfortable room that was a cross between a meeting hall for the Kiwanis Club and an underground bunker.

When Kate and Molly walked up, two men were standing guard duty outside the cellar door entrance, posing nonchalantly, watching for trouble. No one knew how to stand around nonchalantly better than gay men. Almost three hundred people were packed into the windowless space. They lined the walls crammed together on every available inch. Seats were reserved only for the most seriously ill and Kate saw a few young men in various stages of the disease. She also saw many faces she had noticed daily in her neighborhood for years but had never interacted with socially. The majority of the crowd, however, did seem robust and energetic. Fresh juice and extra blankets were available and passed along in a calm manner. In fact, permeating everything was an atmosphere of concern and personal caring combining a variety of styles. Even with that huge crowd everyone got to speak his name.

"John, Jack, Raphael—hi!, Mary, Mary, Bill, Bill, Bill, Sam, Joey—and I'm glad to be here, Dave, Bill, Jean-Yves, Mike, Roberto, El Topo from the BMT, Spin, Wolfman, Bill, Bill, Frank, Pat, Kate, Molly, Bob, Elvis, Cardinal Spellman . . .''

Scott began the meeting with a list of announcements. As he read from the notes he played unconsciously with his ponytail, twisting the hair around the forefinger of his right hand. He had a combined air of enthusiasm and serious determination: like a middle-class boy who one day discovered injustice and then proceeded to do something about it with both sincere conviction and class arrogance about getting things done his way.

"Okay, first, the book *Surviving and Thriving with AIDS* is now available from the People with AIDS Coalition, 263A West 19th Street, room 125, New York, New York 10011. Now, we're trying to convince the supermarkets and Woolworth's to carry it so you just march up to your nearest five-and-dime and tell them you're not buying any more enemas or nail polish until they carry the book."

Whenever he finished an impassioned statement, Scott would look up shyly and flash a big smile. Reassured, he then returned to his list. He also swung his hips a lot because he, like everyone else in the room, was really excited and had a powerful sense of hope.

"Next, AL721 fans. This drug is still not available over the counter, thanks to the boobs at the FDA. But we have batches of lecithin which you can get from us or a number of health food stores. Once you have lecithin you can whip up your own homemade AL721 using this handy recipe that we are passing around the room. Share it with your friends. It goes on your toast in the morning and helps fight those nasty retroviruses."

He smiled again.

"What's next? Oh yes, for those of you who are illegal and don't have green cards, we have a fresh collection of fake birth certificates and passports so you can get Medicaid to pay for your anti-AIDS drugs, as they should, and you can get welfare if you're too sick to work. Remember, the only industrialized nations that do not have socialized medicine are the US of A and South Africa. For more information on fake documents, please see Fabian after the meeting. Fabian, raise your lovely fist so the brothers and sisters know who you are."

Fabian was a longtime leather queen who looked a bit uncomfortable in his khakis, but he kept on a leather cap and slave necklace for old times' sake.

"Remember," Fabian said grinning through his mustache, "S and M is safe sex."

That provoked a round of applause from the impassioned brotherhood.

"That's it for me," Scott said. "Any more announcements?"

Molly's friend Bob jumped up and brushed back his long gray hair. Kate recognized him immediately from the old food co-op.

"Yes, Silver Fox? What do you have for us tonight?"

Bob took his time getting to the front of the room and fluttered like a red leaf or old newspaper caught up in a slowly twirling wind.

"I have an announcement from the Get Real Committee," he said. "For those of you who are new, the Get Real Committee was formed to face reality when everyone else chooses not to. We have made contact with the custodial staff at Riker's Island and we are setting up daily drop-offs of free condoms and clean needles for the fellas and gals inside. Remember this is all unofficial activity, so if you have friends on the inside, either inmates or staff, please pass their names on to me and we can plug them in. Thank you and you're beautiful."

"Thank you, brother Bob. Now, brother James will say a few words about Justice, which will be followed by the business at hand."

James stood up very slowly and walked to the middle of the room wearing a full-length wool sweater dress and a white fur hat.

"That's what happens when queens collide," Bob whispered. "We witness new heights in advanced wardrobe planning."

"You should give him your old femme clothes," Molly murmured in Kate's ear.

He was actually a short man although he had a lot of presence. But he wasn't a preacher and he wasn't a rock star and he wasn't a con man or Prince or our next president. He basically knew how to dress and had clarity.

"The gay community," James said, "is a unique community because our family is bonded on love. Each one of us has defined our lives by love and sexuality—the two greatest human possibilities. We have all recognized these truths in the face of great denial. And now we must use that insight to fight the hypocrisy surrounding the AIDS crisis."

People were sitting very still. They weren't mesmerized, but they were certainly interested.

"When you are diagnosed with AIDS or ARC, or you find out that you are HIV-positive, the normal question is 'How long will I live?' Remember, no one on earth knows the answer to that question, *whether they have AIDS or not*. The fact that you have AIDS, that my lover Scott has AIDS, cannot be changed."

Kate felt her eyes shifting toward Scott.

Then a watch alarm went off.

"Now," James continued. "Let us look at our goals." He wiped his forehead with a lace handkerchief.

"We want prevention, care and cure. But America will never be healthy as long as it exists in a state of advanced hypocrisy. And fate has chosen us to correct this wrong."

Kate looked over at Scott again.

"This week many of you received eviction notices from Ronald Horne's development company. This is the man who has warehoused thousands of empty apartments while ninety thousand people live in the subways and stairwells and public bathrooms of this city. Now we have learned that he has purposely bought buildings with more than fifty percent gay tenants in the hope that we will drop dead and leave him with empty apartments. He files these eviction notices anticipating that some of us will be too ill to contest. Now let me ask you, what are we going to do to get *justice*?"

There was a great steamy silence when he finished, almost

like *subito piano* in music; the quiet after a crescendo, like falling off a cliff.

Men's voices filled the room. Some had constructive ideas. Some just wanted to talk. Some had bad suggestions or feeble ones like "Let's call a lawyer." But almost everyone wanted a chance to speak.

"I say an eye for an eye," called out Cardinal Spellman, a short, bald man with a tiny mustache. "Let's take away his house."

"I have a better idea," called out Bob. "Let's take away his Castle."

That was the spark that united the anger and brought a relatively quiet room to life. No one can ever be as angry when it's hopeless as they can be when there's something to be done about it. People work for change when they think there's a chance of getting it. Otherwise they say, "Why bother?"

Ronald Horne's Castle was the biggest, lushest, most ostentatious and expensive hotel from the Eastern Seaboard to Rodeo Drive. And it was located right in the middle of midtown redevelopment, so the guests could have a clear view of their power and riches at work. It was renowned, not only for its lavishness, but also for the transplanted tropical rain forest that had been re-created inside the lobby to serve as a symbolic moat with actual crocodiles. The guests could feel like authentic aristocracy instead of the robber barons that they really were. From the moment they checked in they were treated like royalty from the middle ages. The motif was Early Modern Colonialism and the staff was required to dress in loincloths with chains hanging from their wrists and ankles. The men's room didn't say Men on the door. It said Bwana. The bathrooms were designed to look like diamond mines with black attendants wearing lanterns and pulling paper towels out with pickaxes. Chicken salad on rye cost twelve dollars.

"We should go now," James said. "We're angry now, so we should go now."

"But how are we going to get cabs for three hundred?" asked a clean-shaven young man in a black leather jacket, who looked like he had a lot of discretionary income.

"I-R-T" began as a steady chant from the back of the room. "I-R-T."

"I think I'm going with them," Kate said. "I haven't done anything like this since the Vietnam War."

"I'm staying here," Molly said. "Fabian and I are going to be on phone duty in case of emergency. Good luck. I hope the trains aren't too delayed."

Kate started to file out the door with this huge group of guys. It took until they got to the Astor Place station before she realized she was the only one in a suit.

27
PETER

▲▲▲

Peter couldn't sleep. Not at all. Where was Kate? She was getting so flamboyant about this. It was out of hand. There was that one night when she hadn't come home at all. Now she was doing that again. How could he face her the next morning sauntering in with someone else's pubic hair between her teeth? He decided to go out for a drink. As he clambered down the stairs Peter hoped he might run into her sneaking up. She'd see how much she had hurt him then. He'd pretend he had some mysterious liaison and it would be her turn to worry. The shoe would be on the other foot then. He even lingered a bit on the ground floor landing, giving her one last chance to catch him leaving.

Peter walked down Second Avenue past endless rows of people selling their stuff on the street. Over the years the quality of goods had diminished. Kate mentioned seeing some good stuff late at night on the way back from the studio, but all he saw was junk. There were so many sellers out even at this hour, mostly standing around trying to keep warm. The lucky ones were drinking pints of wine.

Maybe he'd find a woman at a bar who was lonely too. Maybe he'd stumble home with whiskey on his breath and tell Kate he had been working late. The thought almost made him cry. But by the time he sat down at the bar with a drink in his hand, both of these scenarios seemed equally unlikely. Not knowing what else to do now that he had actually bought the drink, he slouched over the wooden bar and looked at the TV.

"You want to buy a gold chain?" some guy breathed down his neck. "Fourteen-karat."

"No thanks," Peter mumbled, slumping even further.

On TV there was a man talking. If he didn't pay close attention to the precise words Peter would have no idea of what he was trying to communicate because the man had no facial expressions and modulated all phrases with an absolutely identical cadence.

"Who's that?" he asked the bartender, a short Polish guy smoking Barclay's. "Is that the president?"

"Nah," the guy said, sucking as hard as he could on the cig, trying to get more flavor than it had to give. "That's the anchorman."

Mr. Anchor had a maudlin yellow glow over his skin, which was made of wax.

"Since when is there TV news on at one thirty in the morning?" Peter asked, trying to establish some kind of camaraderie with the bartender, who kept resisting.

"It's cable, buddy. Where have you been? They got news twenty-four hours a day now. They got a whole station that plays nothing but sports and one only for stocks and one only for music videos. You don't have to switch channels anymore, looking for what you want. Now you know what is where all night long."

"TV is so shocking," said Peter, "when you don't watch it for a while. Why would anyone want to believe a guy who looks like that? He's in terrible shape and he's got on too much pancake. Look at him. His skin is the texture of stale dough."

The commercials were more impressive, however. They were actually well done.

"Not bad," Peter had to admit. "Not bad at all."

"In tonight's news," said the anchorman, "AIDS."

"Oooh, I'm so sick of AIDS," Peter groaned. He couldn't help himself.

"Fuck you," said the gay man sitting next to him with a bottle of beer. "Sorry to spoil your party but people are suffering, you know."

"I know. You're right. I'm sorry. It's just that my wife is going gay, you see. And all I hear about nowadays is gay this and gay that. But you're absolutely right. I apologize."

He ordered another drink. Only when it came did he realize how nauseated he felt.

"Hundreds of AIDS victims have occupied the restaurant and lobby of Ronald Horne's Castle in midtown Manhattan. They are demanding that the superstar developer rescind eviction notices sent to homosexual men in Horne-owned buildings. Many of the hotel guests have fled in terror, especially those from the Sunbelt region. Some are angrily demanding refunds and immediate AIDS tests. Mr. Horne remains unavailable for comment from his retreat in Hawaii, where he and his lovely wife Lucretia are vacationing with Imelda and Ferdinand Marcos. But Castle spokesman Bill Smith did speak earlier with Channel Z."

The camera zoomed in on a blustering red-faced gentleman wearing a grass skirt and a fuchsia lei, carrying a six-foot bullwhip.

"Tell us, Mr. Smith, is this your usual attire?"

"Why yes. Mr. Horne prefers that all management dress like tropical overseers so the guests can feel more comfortable and secure."

"Mr. Smith, as a representative of the Horne dynasty, can you tell our television audience how you think this demonstration will affect future business transactions at the Castle?"

"I want to assure all future guests," he said, waving the whip for emphasis, "that all glassware and eating utensils will be replaced as soon as we clear the lobby. We expect the New York Police Department imminently."

The camera panned the crowd a bit, stopping in front of the black man that Peter had seen calling out at the cathedral.

"Tell us, sir," said the persistently plastic reporter, "who is going to pay for all this damage?"

"The hotel was built on tax rebates," James said through a huge grin. In the background Peter could see crowds of gay men laughing, dancing and popping champagne corks. "We've already paid."

The camera went back to the crowd. It looked like the Mets' locker room after they won the World Series. Men were in varying states of revelry, sharing drinks at the bar, singing show tunes in the piano lounge, watching old movies on the huge video screen, conversing intensely in the smoking room. And they were all snacking on caviar and smoked oysters.

"Oh, no," said Peter out loud, unable to control himself.

"What's the matter now, asshole?" yelled the gay man at the bar. "I've had it with you heteros. You don't care about anyone but yourselves."

"No, it's not you," Peter said, barely able to get out the words. "It's my wife."

"What do you mean?" asked the bartender, whose interest had been piqued. "There's all guys there."

"No, that's her. The redhead with the crew cut in a suit and tie. That's my wife."

"This is some world," said the bartender. "But you gotta live and let live. Fucking faggots."

There she was. You couldn't miss her. That orange hair looked more mandarin on the eerie color TV. She was in earnest conversation with a tall man brushing out a silver mane of hair and braiding it into pigtails.

" 'Nother round?" the bartender asked and poured it without waiting for confirmation.

"You may ask," resumed the reporter in the classic frontal electronic journalism pose, staring sincerely at his public, "where are the police? Well, according to Chief of Command Ed Ramsey of Manhattan South, his officers are not properly equipped to come into contact with large numbers of AIDS victims."

"Not *victim*, you breeder," screamed the gay man at the bar, who clearly couldn't take it anymore. "*People with AIDS* is the appropriate term." He dropped his head down on the bar and closed his eyes.

The reporter, however, continued as though at any moment he would say, "But first, the sports."

"The police have put in emergency requisitions for rubber gloves and are waiting patiently for the supplies to arrive. This is Roland Johnson for Channel Z. More later, but first, the sports."

When the picture switched to Mike Tyson and Robin Givens, the gay man next to Peter took out his Walkman.

"Hold on, I can get WBAI."

He listened intently and then reported each piece of information to the inebriated bar.

"It took the police forever to get rubber gloves," he shouted, constantly fidgeting with the dial. "They originally requisitioned them from the Veterans' Hospital and the BAI guy interviewed someone from the VA saying they don't even have sheets or pillows, how could the police expect to find a roomful of extra rubber gloves lying around. . . . Oh shit."

"What's the matter now?" asked the bartender.

"It's marathon week. They've stopped reporting the news until they get fifteen new subscribers. Turn on the television set."

Everyone resumed their places at the bar with a new round of drinks, eyes glued to the tube.

28
MOLLY

▲▲

Molly and Fabian spent the whole night listening to the radio. Once BAI announced their number as control central they started fielding calls from all corners. Mostly it was gay people from the five boroughs wanting subway directions and asking for updates.

There appeared to be a standoff for a while when the cops couldn't get their rubbers, but finally Overseer Smith personally commissioned three slaves to run out to a number of all-night drugstores and buy fifty pairs of Playtex Living Gloves, which turned out to be an unfortunate lemon yellow. It made the overweight cops look sillier than necessary, reported Bob from a pay phone in the lobby.

"They resemble advertisements for dishwashing soap, or more appropriately, ducks."

The demonstrators, being in top form, took immediate advantage of this new situation by chanting "Your gloves don't match your shoes" as they walked out the front door, avoiding arrest altogether. This was actually a relief to the police, Bob thought, because they clearly had no idea of where they could put three hundred prisoners with AIDS anyway. Once outside, they lined up and serenaded Mr. Smith, who had climbed up a coconut tree for safety. Then they left the place completely depleted of roasted nuts and Courvoisier VSOP. Justice's name rang throughout the land and Kate came back and took Molly to bed.

"This has been a very important night for me," she said. "It's given me a lot of ideas." Then she said, "I want to speak all this love to you but I'm too shy."

"Like what?"

"Like *sweetie* and *baby*. But not *baby* as in *baby talk*. But more romantic and sensual, on an island beach with passion and warm cool breezes."

"Sounds all right to me."

"You know," Kate said, stretching back so her arms looked like branches of a madrona tree. "I worry a lot about being alone."

Molly turned over on her stomach and licked those open spaces behind Kate's ears. Her head was practically shaved, leaving a slightly orange hue over her shell-pink scalp.

"Kate, what if you're like me and you don't have someone there all the time?"

"Then in your thirties you'll feel like an outcast but in your forties you'll get your revenge."

"Why?" Molly asked, running her fingers over Kate's nipples.

"That's when everyone else's security shatters but only you know how to live on your own. They're helpless. They can't eat a meal by themselves or go to a movie solo without seeing it as a symbol of misery."

"So, Kate, are you telling me that I'm destined to always be alone?"

"Please, Molly, I love you."

They started making love again in a violet haze where their features were close and very smooth. Kate was really working at it, all muscle and sinew, grunting and sweating, climbing across her body. When they were lying quietly in their own sweat, Kate pointed out Molly's window.

"The sun is coming up and there are birds everywhere. How unusual."

29
PETER

△△△

One morning Peter and Kate lay in bed for a long time. He rubbed her feet and cleaned out her toenails before clipping them. He oiled her legs and breasts until she smelled like a baby and then he rubbed her shoulders and the back of her neck. Then they made love. It was all physical. No talking. He made her a cup of coffee and held her closely under his arm and next to his body as they walked to her studio in the spring rain.

"You're so sweet," she said. "To take such good care of me."

They talked about painting the living room and which color would be the best, which store would be the best to buy it from and which day of the week would be the best to get the job done. They discussed a new restaurant that had opened on the block and each gave their opinion of the decor. Peter mentioned an article he had read in *New German Critique* and Kate told about an exhibit at PPOW Gallery she had dropped in on accidentally while trying to find something else. It was the murmurings and patterns of speech that were familiar. The actual information was just another way to share and fill time.

Peter felt a pure satisfaction. It had been too long since he had walked down the street with Kate held firmly in his arm. Lately they had walked to and from various theatrical events with a distracted sense of habit and compulsive conversation about things no one really had to say, but someone was there and so you said them. But on this spring day Peter knew that they were in love and deeply bonded.

"Here we are."

She turned to kiss him good-bye in the drizzle and he felt the heat of her body through her dark flannel trousers.

"When we were making love and I went inside you," he said, "I could feel that you were on fire, inside, and you were gripping me, drawing me into the hot core."

She didn't answer.

Peter stood in the rain watching her walk into the building and he felt warm and sexual. He knew that everything was going to be corrected and set off for work.

The show he was designing was called *The Malling of America*, a musical about urban sprawl. It took place in a vaguely Midwestern city that required three shades of gray and one sharp blue. Then he decided to add some sickly pink to stand in for the car exhaust. These generic cities, Peter knew, were ugly clumps of buildings hacked apart by the inevitable interstate. Putting highways through the middle of cities was the urban equivalent of strip-mining. It bored a hole in something organic that could never be repaired. The light had to reflect the lack of clarity, everything under a huge shadow. There would be no natural light, just stores with neon and fluorescent show windows with cars constantly whizzing by, a light source in perpetual motion.

Today he needed to work in the theater and compare the available instruments with the room's possibilities. It shouldn't take more than a few hours. Then he could get in a quick workout at the gym and be home for Kate.

He stepped into the theater, a one-hundred-seater in the West Twenties. Everything was adequate but nothing spectacular. The ceiling was too low, but it was only those fiberglass panels which were easily removable, but what a mess.

"Hello, Peter."

He looked up. It was Robert, that young intern from Yale.

"I'm working with you again," he said unflappably. "I've been hired on to this project."

Then he swung that same briefcase up on the tabletop and popped open the steel clasps with a snap.

Same moves, Peter noticed. *But with a different kind of edge this time. Maybe his girlfriend finally broke up with him.*

"Nice to see you, Robert. We are going to have a fun project ahead of us here. A complicated one. This is city light, not natural light and so every source is a human invention and decision complicated by circumstance. We have to justify all the placements and intensities with the story of the man who installed them that way. You'll see. We'll have fun. How many fluorescent lights are in how many offices? How many of those are blinking, or simply out? How many drivers are on the interstate that cuts through town? How many turned on their brights?"

"Good," Robert said, flatly, soberly distracted. "I'm ready to work." Then he held out his hand to Peter, offering him a formal handshake.

What's this? Peter thought, but took hold for no reason. Then the young man seemed to crumple in Peter's hand, beginning with the wrist and losing power systematically like an inflatable skeleton.

"I'm sorry," Robert said, not wiping his tears on the sleeve of his jacket, but instead producing a perfectly folded, white, ironed handkerchief in which he blew his nose. Then he stopped crying by pressing his thumb and forefinger against the ridge of his nose and shutting his eyes so tightly that no water could seep out.

"My father's lover died yesterday."

"Oh," Peter said, very uncomfortable. Then he said, "I'm sorry."

"Let's get to work," Robert said, regaining full composure. He took off his suit jacket, hung it carefully over the back of his chair and folded up his sleeves. "It's the best way to feel better."

"You're a real artist then," Peter said, feeling that was the best comfort he could give.

First they counted lights and checked the bulbs to see precisely what they had to play with. They put up some basic piping for the hang. The room was small enough that Peter could size up fairly quickly what he'd be needing, and he looked forward to plotting it all out more precisely that evening at his desk.

"Do you mind if I tell you what it was about him that I liked the best?" Robert asked as they were wrapping and labeling cable.

"Sure."

"Well, Curtis really was my friend. He wasn't a parent and he wasn't just Dad's boyfriend. He was my friend because he was for me. We didn't agree all the time but he wanted me to make the right decisions. But when I made the wrong ones he still cared about me."

Robert found a split piece of cable and started wrapping it with gaffer's tape. He took out brand-new scissors from their special carrying container built into the briefcase.

"When someone gets sick like that," he said, "it makes them decide what they really want from their life."

Peter felt a twinge of anxiety.

"And what they really have, you mean."

"No," Robert said, convinced. "It's more what they have always wanted but have continuously put off for another day. Of course, that is all dependent on whether or not they can accept what is happening to their body."

There was something so threatening in Robert's voice that Peter felt terrified. He felt his throat constrict. When he intended to answer with a typically jovial response, there was no sound. He saw white. He felt cold. Kate was ruining everything. Things were so nice between them today, why did she have to stay with that little bitch? Peter started having pictures in his brain of ideas that weren't relevant. If ever Kate was in a hospital he would have to fight for time with that other one. If Kate were ever really sick, he would have to do whatever she wanted and wait out in the corridor like a punished schoolgirl while the two of them sat giggling.

Peter felt afraid from being so out of control. Then he felt furious. Something in what Robert had said reminded him of his loneliness. It reminded him of his helplessness. It told him he was alone. He was sad. He had no friends and no one to take care of him. He had no one to take care of him because he had been abandoned. He was abandoned and overprotected. He was given everything and nothing. It had ruined him. It had made him awkward. Now he was vulnerable as a result. He was lost. He was a lost boy who could not cry. He was hurt and soft. He was soft like a woman but he was not a woman. A woman left you when you were down. She had an affair when you were vulnerable. If he had not been vulnerable he would have had an affair too, but he was so he couldn't.

"Are you all right?" Robert asked, trying not to look worried. "Do you need to take a walk outside in the air?"

"You know, Robert," Peter said. "It's not as easy to be a man as it once was. Actually it never was easy and now it's worse than before. People blame you for everything. But all along you have to keep your perspective. You have to keep your balance."

Peter stood up and took a deep breath. He stretched out his muscular arms and touched his toes. He was in good shape.

"This is New York City," he said. "The best thing is to focus on the big picture. Just take the long view and don't get dragged down in temporary details. Do you see what I mean?"

"No," Robert said. "I don't see it that way at all."

30

PETER

ΔΔΔΔΔΔΔΔΔΔΔΔΔΔΔΔΔΔΔΔΔΔΔΔΔΔΔΔΔΔΔΔΔΔΔΔΔΔΔΔΔΔΔΔΔΔΔΔΔΔΔΔΔΔΔΔΔΔΔΔΔΔΔΔΔΔΔΔ

It was clearly spring but there were still knives in the air when the rain came down too strong and cold and the wind whipped too fast. Peter felt the rain beating against his waterproof coat. He was protected. The sky was silver like the coat and the buildings.

Heading downtown he passed a line of street people not being too rowdy. They were waiting to get into a soup kitchen set up by a local synagogue. He watched them closely. They were mostly black. They had survived the winter. Some seemed disoriented but he couldn't tell if they were homeless because they were confused, like the TV said, or if being homeless had driven them insane, which seemed a lot more likely. But they didn't all show very dramatic emotions. Some were just quietly down on their luck. A couple of the younger guys had a lot of energy and were either joking around or antagonizing one another. They danced by the older men who looked blank and rubbed huge

ΔΔΔΔΔΔΔΔΔΔΔΔΔΔΔΔΔΔΔΔΔΔΔΔΔΔΔΔΔΔΔΔΔΔΔΔΔΔΔΔΔΔΔΔΔΔΔΔΔΔΔΔΔΔΔΔΔΔΔΔ hands over their entire heads and faces like they were oh so tired. No one was properly dressed. The few women were mostly quite thin, some with babies or younger children. None of whom looked older than eight. The moms were skinny and some had that junkie/crackhead zombie look with sunken or distracted eyes and missing teeth. Peter figured that the ones who were better organized probably still had somewhere to stay but not enough food, so they had to stand out in the rain with their kids. But he didn't know for sure if that was true. There were also some traditional bag ladies who were overweight and wearing and carrying a lot of stuff. They spoke loudly and had a lot to say. The skinny ones just tried to keep their kids quiet.

When he started looking at these people, Peter felt a deep, deep compassion. It drew him closer to them, this sense of injustice that they had been treated so badly. He crossed the street and was practically next to them, watching everyone file inside. Then he followed. Once through the door Peter discovered that these people had been waiting for soup and coffee and cheese and peanut butter and jelly on white bread sandwiches. Then he saw a whole table of elderly people, mostly white and black with two Chinese couples. They kept away from the drug addicts and winos and bag ladies and down-on-their-luck men. The elderly people liked to eat quietly and slowly. The other people ate fast, then sat back and stared.

Peter stood against the back wall watching everything. He was the only one in the room with rain boots. He was the only blond. People drank their coffee very slowly out of Styrofoam cups, like they knew how to make a cup of coffee last an afternoon. That way it didn't matter how quickly they ate their sandwiches. The smell in the room was overpoweringly bad. But it wasn't the room itself, it was the people in it. The warmer the room became, the more he could smell rotting flesh and urine.

When the meal was over, another group of people came into the room. They were all white, mostly aging, but well cared-for. The men wore a relaxed collection of suits while the women had black skirts of all styles with a variety of nice blouses. They lined up in three rows at the front of the room and a young gay rabbi spoke into the microphone.

"Welcome ladies and gentlemen. Congregation Beth Shalom welcomes you to our community food program. Today we have a special program for you in honor of Passover, the Festival of Liberation. The temple's resident Jewish Folk Chorus has offered to sing for you. Please welcome this wonderful group under the direction of Irv Jacobson."

Nobody applauded. Most people were still sitting over their coffee and didn't pay any attention. The ones who appeared to be listening were actually just staring.

Then Irv stepped up to conduct. He was wearing two hearing aids. He turned to face the audience.

"Our first two songs are dear to the hearts of the . . ."

"Louder! Louder!" yelled one of the bag ladies with three coats. But Irv didn't hear.

"Irv," the women in the front line of the chorus started to say under their breath. Then they got louder. "Irv! Irv!"

They were tugging at his jacket, trying to get his attention.

"What?"

"They can't hear you."

"They can't hear me?"

"Use the microphone."

So he walked over to the microphone and started talking.

"This next song is dear to the hearts of the Jewish people."

The mike blinked out immediately but Irv couldn't tell. He was too deaf and kept on talking.

"Irv," the women in the first row of the chorus started again. "Irv, Irv, they can't hear you. It's not working."

"I thought it was working."

"Let's just sing, Irv."

He raised his hands and they started to sing "Alle Menschen Sienen Brider" and Irv had an expression of euphoria on his face.

Peter looked around the room. With the exception of the bag lady who yelled, "Go, Irv," no one cared one way or the other about the Jewish Folk Chorus. The best you could say was that some of them didn't mind. Except for the old people at the separate table. They were happy. They couldn't sing along because they didn't know the language but they realized that someone was going out of their way for them and Irv was in such rapture that some of the old people felt his pleasure vicariously. It made them remember something about their own songs which seemed very important right then.

Peter stood there this whole time, rain dripping from his raincoat. Everyone else's clothes were soaked through, but his were dry.

How can you relieve suffering for even one moment? he thought. *Here we are, the homeless, the old, the artists. The sadness is so overwhelming I can't imagine what to do. Nothing in my life has prepared me for this.*

31

PETER

ΔΔΔΔΔΔΔΔΔΔΔΔΔΔΔΔΔΔΔΔΔΔΔΔΔΔΔΔΔΔΔΔΔΔΔΔΔΔΔΔΔΔΔΔΔΔΔΔΔΔΔΔΔΔΔΔΔΔΔΔΔΔΔΔΔΔΔΔΔΔΔ

By five o'clock Kate still hadn't come home, so he called her studio and got the recording. He sat at his desk working on the lighting plot until eleven and then called the studio again. Still a recording. So he decided to go over to the studio.

It was really pouring and Peter wore his boots and raincoat and carried an umbrella. He liked to be well protected from the weather. He didn't like to get wet and it was easy to stay dry if you just took the time to put on all the necessary accessories. In New Hampshire, when it snowed, the ground reflected the moonlight and everything was clearly illuminated, even without stars. Sometimes in the day it was so bright, it hurt your eyes. But Peter could start at the top of the hill and roll down the whole way without getting hurt because the snow was so deep and soft and people knew how to dress warmly up there.

"Hey man, could you help me out?"

Peter turned and saw a tall wiry black man wearing a ski

hat pulled so low over his forehead it covered his eyebrows. The man looked him straight in the eye.

"Sure," he said reaching into his pockets and handing the man fifty cents.

"Thanks. Now I need help with this."

He held up his hand. It was so huge and scarred and dry that it had cracked open many times over a few years. There was a kind of green tinge that had overtaken much of it, except for a section obscured by a dirty bandage and tape. It looked a little bit like one of those monster hands kids buy at Woolworth's for Halloween. The man was very upset. He was almost crying.

"I went to Bellevue," he said, "and they wrapped it up. But then they gone and give me this."

He pulled out a wrinkled prescription from his back pocket. His pants were so thin Peter could see every muscle twitch underneath them.

"They tell me to fill it, but they don't tell me how. Now it's late and everything is closed and I still didn't get my medicine."

"Let me see."

Peter looked at the piece of paper. It looked legitimate. The guy seemed to be actually hurt. The whole thing was on the level.

"Okay," Peter said. "Let's find a pharmacy. I'll show you how to fill a prescription and then the next time you need something you'll know how to do it on your own."

They walked along at a fast pace. The guy was Peter's age. *That's too old to be out on the street,* he thought.

"I don't want to lose my hand," the guy said.

"Is that what they told you at Bellevue?"

"No, but I just got that feeling."

It's really important that two men from different circumstances can communicate like this, Peter thought. Then he wondered if the guy was just laying it on thick, trying to get some money out of him.

"Well, don't worry," Peter said. "There's a pharmacy right up the block."

But when they got there it was closed.

"There's another one about three blocks away. Can you make it?"

"Yeah."

They almost ran to that one, both of them sweating in the damp, wet night. They raced right up to the front door before accepting that it was locked.

"Let me ask that cop," Peter said, wondering exactly what he had gotten himself into.

"No, no cops," the man said, grabbing the paper out of Peter's hand.

"Okay," Peter said. His head was swimming. He felt trapped, like an outlaw. What should he do? Should he call a cab to take them to an all-night pharmacy? Should he just give the guy ten bucks? It was getting very late. Was this all a scam to get ten bucks out of him? Then he looked up and saw Molly walking down the street. She wasn't wearing a raincoat. She didn't have on boots or a rain hat or an umbrella. She wore her jacket collar up and hunched her shoulders against the rain.

"Molly."

She looked up, acknowledged him, but definitely kept on walking.

"Molly, help me, will you?"

She stopped then and stepped in under his umbrella so that they were very close. The guy was standing under the awning of a deli, looking both ways at all times.

"What's the matter, Peter?"

"This guy stopped me. He needs to get a prescription filled but all the pharmacies are closed and I'm not sure of what to do. Do you know of an open pharmacy?"

She looked at the prescription.

"Tylenol Three. That's a painkiller. It has codeine."

"Oh," he said.

Then she walked over to the guy standing under the awning. "Do you need a painkiller?"

"Yes I do."

"How much does it hurt?"

"It hurts. It aches. It's sore. I need to stop the pain."

"Then what are you going to do?" she asked him, not sympathetically, but with a challenge in her voice, like she expected to hear the correct answer to that question.

She's so aggressive, Peter thought. *You'd think she'd have a little more heart for a guy in trouble. It's probably because he's a man.*

"I don't know."

"Look, we'll get you something now, but you have to go back in the hospital tomorrow morning and tell them to look at it again. Do you have Medicaid?"

"I don't have a card."

"Wait here."

She walked into the deli, avoiding Peter, not discussing any of it with him. Then she came out with a bottle of Tylenol, a pack of Marlboros and two quarts of Budweiser.

"Take six of these and drink these and you'll numb out for a while."

The guy took everything and split. He ran away. He didn't want to be around them anymore.

Peter and Molly looked at each other. They had to.

"How are you?" Peter said.

"I've been really busy," Molly said. "I've been doing a lot of organizing work."

"Oh really?" Peter said. "Are you a secretary?"

He saw her mouth open like she was going to say a specific thing, but then she decided to say something else instead.

"You can only do so much for people you don't love," she said. "There are a lot of deprived people in this city. You have to know where they stop and you begin."

"But maybe I should have taken him to Bellevue in a cab," Peter said, looking down the empty street. "Or I could have tried a few more places. There must be an all-night drugstore somewhere in Manhattan."

He watched the droplets of rain drip off her nose and down her neck. She didn't even try to step out of it.

"Well, you could have done that, but at some point you would have to say *stop.* You weren't going to take him home with you and give him a pair of your pajamas, were you?"

"I was just trying to help someone," he said.

"Yes, I know," she said. "I'm sure you're a very nice person."

The rain was noisy. It smelled good. The next day would be

fresh. There would be buds on the trees on Saint Mark's Place.

"My personal life is falling apart," Peter said. "I'm balding."

"Well, you could get a little tattoo, like a shooting star on your temple. It would fill in your hairline. Besides, people would be so busy looking at your tattoo they would forget that you were losing your hair."

He didn't want her to leave.

"When I first saw you I couldn't understand why Kate would be attracted, but now that I've watched you moving around, I can see why she's interested."

"Oh no," Molly said.

"I know you think I'm a macho hetero," he said, feeling sort of masculine at that moment. "But I have a real problem with your separatism."

"My what?"

"Your separatism. You see, I think people are all the same. But you want to run around in gay-this and gay-that. You know, Molly, men are people too. People have rights even if they're not gay."

"You can't take anything that isn't about you, can you?"

"What?" he said. He hadn't heard her properly.

"I understand what you're saying," Molly answered, changing her body language, like she had got very tired all of a sudden. "I don't agree, but I know exactly where you're coming from and I understand precisely what you mean."

Peter was so happy right then that he grabbed both of her shoulders and kissed her on the mouth, pulling her body toward him. She barely stood there after that, didn't even give him a full look, just turned and walked away too slowly, not noticing the rain at all. Not looking back.

Peter was elated. He had made friends with his wife's affair. Who could be more flexible and easygoing than that? He knew this would make Kate proud of him.

Peter went directly to her studio. It was long after midnight. He stopped across the street and bought a bouquet of flowers from an all-night fruit stand. Tulips. Tulips in the middle of March. Were they in season? That was New York. You could buy a kiwi fruit at two in the morning any day of the year without going more than three blocks. He picked out deep purples and reds with black lines running through the petals. They were almost opened. He could picture Kate, white and fruity against the dark purple as she pressed the flowers to her face.

"They look so much better when you hold them," he would say. Then he took out his copy of her keys and climbed the stairs.

"What are you doing, Katie? It's late."

She was sitting on the floor with long gray sheets of plastic in her lap. She was painting on them from a little glass jar.

He came closer, but not too close, and knelt down reaching toward her with the top of his body only.

"What are you painting on?"

"Two kinds of X rays," she said, never looking up once. "These in my hand are plain films. For a tumor to be seen on plain film it must be big enough and it must be more dense than the surrounding normal tissue."

"And those?"

"Those are contrast films. That's when they inject dye into you. The contrast film relates to the paint differently than the plain film. It practically rejects it."

She looked up then. She stood, leaving Peter crouching underneath her. Then he stood up as well.

"Aren't you tired, Katie? Don't you want to sleep some?"

"No," she said. "This is the last piece. When I put this in, *People in Trouble* will be almost finished. I'll just have to mount it on the wooden boards and polyurethane the sections and it will be ready for installation."

Then they held each other very tightly. But a close embrace is never the last moment between two people. The last moment is the release and so much more emotion shows then.

32
KATE

△△

The cashier in the Chinese restaurant was listening to a preparatory cassette for her green-card interview. The windows were fogged with pork grease pouring out of the kitchen, but the front door was open too, so spring came in in bits and pieces. Kate and Molly got buzzed on the sunshine and too much Chinese tea.

"Are you willing to take the full oath of allegiance to the United States of America?" asked the authoritative male voice with a mid-Atlantic accent, speaking on tape. He had no intonation.

"Yes," said the woman automatically, rolling chopped meat into dumpling dough. Her teenage daughter was chewing on the edge of a pencil, going back and forth from her calculator to her notebook at one of the empty tables.

"Are you willing to bear arms for the United States?"

"Yes," she said.

"Have you ever sold drugs?"

"Sewed drugs?" she repeated with some doubt.

"Prostitution?" said the tape.

"Pastu shin?" she said, again quizzically.

"Adultery?" said the tape.

"Adol?" she said.

"No!" screamed her daughter. "Sold drugs! Prostitution! Adultery! Adultery! Adultery!"

They both cracked up laughing then and inhaled in unison before returning to their separate tasks.

"When we were making love this afternoon," Kate said, tracing the veins on the inside of Molly's wrist, "I felt my hand almost completely inside you and I could touch a ball of fire, a hot core. Then you gripped me and brought me deeper into the heat."

"What do you like best about me?" Molly asked.

"There is a sky below," Kate said. "And a pair of jeans, a calico rose in the middle of your skull. A red mask. A red egg. A moonscape made of glass. Magnified tongue cells, salted spongy things, mountains of black. Gray hills."

"I'm so happy," Molly said. "This is great. This is like sitting next to a waterfall. This is Paradise Now."

They turned the corner at 103rd Street and walked into the lobby of Mount Sinai Hospital, where Scott had been for the last few days. It wasn't his first time there, and it wasn't his first complication. James had called around welcoming visitors since Scott felt too isolated, not seeing familiar faces.

He was propped up in bed with his hair brushed out loose around his shoulders. He looked like a Madonna, even though his skin was coming apart.

For Kate there was no more sun, there was no more closeness. There was only this other world with two distinct smells: ammonia clean and filthy, stinking dirty. It was hard to believe this raw, bleeding skin was Scott and not just something laid on top of him. She had known, intellectually, that once someone's immune system was shot, every little thing became something enormous. But she had breezed into the hospital room without having accepted that she was going to visit the first friend of hers who would probably die of AIDS.

Funny, she thought. Cancer used to be this big dramatic event. Now, with people dropping dead, cancer is just another thing.

She looked at Scott. Only a month before, all four of them had eaten dinner together at the guys' apartment. Scott's two daughters had been over too, spending the weekend.

He had done all the cooking and serving up the plates. Then the girls bowed their heads for grace so Molly and Kate followed.

"May we each have everything we need and want, immediately, plus self-determination for all people. Amen."

"I was married for four years," Scott told them over dinner that night. "Now we live three blocks from my ex-wife's so I can be near my girls. Greta is seven and Andrea is nine."

While he was speaking James helped Andrea to some food and made sure that Greta didn't get sauce all over her clothes.

"Dad?" Andrea said with a mouthful of food.

"What?"

"Can a kid be brought up to be antigay and still be gay?"

"Yes," he said.

"How come?"

"Because," Scott answered, patting her long hair, wrapping it over her ears and away from her face. "Because people don't become what they were brought up to be, people become themselves."

That night as they sat and talked, Scott and James looked so happy together. They couldn't help but be close and touch from time to time, until James gave into his feelings and curled up in his boyfriend's arms. Kate saw Molly watching her during all of this. At the same time Kate was watching herself. She was seeing herself as part of gay coupling, socializing as a lesbian, watching two men in love with no need for restraint or nervousness. She had become part of their natural environment. And vice versa, almost.

"I've been reading a lot of books about catastrophic human

disasters," James said. He was a social worker for the Jewish Board of Child and Family Service, but he said he got a lot of reading done traveling back and forth on the subway every day.

"I've read books about the plague, about the Holocaust, about Hiroshima, slavery, apartheid. I have read every novel about AIDS that the publishers can get into the stores and it's all unsatisfactory in the same way."

"What way?" It had never occurred to Kate that there were actually novels about AIDS.

"When a person faces death," James said, "especially a deliberate, uncalled-for and avoidable death, they only seem to have two reactions. *Why me?* and *I don't want to die.*"

"What about the philosophers of the Holocaust, for example, like Primo Levi?"

"Those are survivors," he said. "I'm talking about facing death. The only reaction we can really have is a banal one because death is the last experience of life. It's not like love. There is no retrospect. The challenge is to turn it from an overwhelming personal void into a group effort, to try to help others avoid the same fate. But this kind of extraordinary response means agitating against the grain of the habit of human reaction."

Sitting in Scott's hospital room, those ideas seemed completely inadequate as far as Kate was concerned. This man was dying. The more she focused on it, the more out of control she felt. But he was smiling and turning his head. He was talking to her.

"Excuse me?"

"Kate, I said, did you see the newspaper today?"

She read aloud to them from the *Times* op-ed page.

" 'Of course homosexuals are in distress, but they have to learn how to achieve their ends through legislative process. These marauding vigilantes using the misnomer Justice are in blatant violation of the values upon which this nation is built.' "

Scott beamed at that one. Then Molly reached over and brushed his hair off his forehead with her hand. Kate thought about touching that kind of skin.

"Scott," Molly said, "I brought you some supplies for entertaining guests. Here are two kinds of caviar: black and red. And two boxes of Carr's wheat biscuits. Also a bottle of champagne for the starving masses of friends."

"You know," Scott said, "it's much easier having visitors who are used to seeing their friends sickly and weak, because there's no expression of shock on their faces when they walk in and see me. In fact, they look relieved. What's more, everyone has perfected such elegant bedside manners. After visiting a couple of different friends you figure out creative things to bring to the hospital instead of that endless procession of nervous flowers that leave you lying in state when they get excessive."

The room was decorated with rainbow balloons, pictures of Scott and James kissing, drawings and paintings by the girls. He was surrounded by images of loving and hugging and dancing— all the happiest moments of life. A cassette deck was playing Betty Carter and Scott was in the middle of it in his baby blue pajamas with surfboards and blond men playing volleyball.

"What kind of treatment are you going with?" Kate asked, finally relaxed enough to talk. She had never seen anyone so young dying before.

"Well," he said, very evenly. "There are these aerosols of pentamidine, but they don't know how much you need to take or how often. I'm having trouble now with the skin on my chest and face and arms. It's starting to come apart. But they are giving me sunlamp treatments which will not only hold my body together but I get a tan on top of it."

"They should change the name of this place to Mount Sinai Club Med," Molly said.

"You know," Scott said. "You can heal yourself or you can't. I'm trying the best I can, but you know what? It's very hard. It's really very hard."

33

KATE

△△△

The subway station was a mess and too disorienting after the hospital. Brown garbage was piled on the stairs and had to be stepped over gingerly like small rocks across a creek. There was a seemingly endless, faceless sea of beggars standing or sitting on many of the steps, ranging from a nine-year-old panhandler/pickpocket to a nun with an upturned tambourine packed with change. Every single seat on the platform had a person sleeping in it.

The first car they stepped into had homeless people stretched out on the benches and in all four corners. They moved into the second car.

"You know," Kate said, putting her arm around Molly in the little double seat by the sliding doors, "the main thing that I have learned from being with you is that I am a growing, changing person. But I don't really understand your politics. Don't try to explain them again either. There's just something I absolutely do not comprehend about what the big deal is at the core of your world view."

Molly laid her head against Kate's shoulder and periodically closed and opened her eyes as the train sped downtown.

Molly's always in motion, Kate thought, watching her. *But slowly, like t'ai chi.* It wasn't movement in the extremities but the constant shifts in weight, gaze and position. The face was always changing. It was hard to get a fixed image of what it really looked like. If Kate turned away and looked back conventionally, as one would in conversation, it would never be the same woman. But if Kate was bold and happy and they let themselves look at each other fully, then Kate could see all the changes in one frame. It was something like that speeded-up film of the opening of a flower. There was no particular image in any stationary moment, just the shift that became important. *It is that change,* Kate thought, settling into the rumbling of the subway car, *that I recall when I think of her.*

"Kate, I was remembering about a weird thing." Molly pulled her knapsack onto her lap. "When Pearl and I were still a couple, one weekend we went for a vacation upstate. We checked into a redneck hotel run by Ukrainians up near Lexington, New York, where Pearl lives now. She walked up to the owner that time and asked for a double bed, even though I had specifically begged her not to. You know, I intend to live to be thirty. But Pearl must have things exactly the way she wants them at all moments regardless of the danger. So then I was scared the whole first night, wouldn't raise the curtains to let in the moonglow, wouldn't make love with the light on. I was sure I saw something hovering by the window. Plus, she makes loud noises during sex and the next morning the desk clerk smirked right in our faces. His wife, who ran the coffee shop next door, was icy cold and didn't say a word."

Molly found the lotion she was looking for and rubbed it onto her hands. Kate could smell the cucumber.

"I was used to smirks but began to suspect more serious troubles when this group of three men who were also eating breakfast decided to befriend us, with winks to the owner watching from the corner. I wanted to get out of there but we only had a couple of days and it would have ruined everything to have to pack up and go shopping for a new place. When we came back from the woods they were all there having supper. That's when we found out that one of the guys was working as the clerk that night. The other two started pressuring us to drive with them to Hunter to go to a disco."

A man whose feet were wrapped in filthy rags staggered in at the Forty-second street station. There were also two teenage boys who seemed borderline emaciated. The boys had thin jackets and sat silently huddled. The man immediately stretched out to sleep on the seats across from the two women. Molly was rubbing lotion into both hands and lifting them to her face and neck.

"I didn't want to go out with them and I didn't war t to dance with men."

Kate winced.

"Why do you always have to say something bad about men? Maybe they were nice men. Maybe they were good dancers."

"I just don't like to dance with straight men. I'm not going to pretend I do. I don't care whether I'm attractive to them or not. I don't want to hear about it."

Kate knew that this was a direct dig against Peter.

"So anyway, we said, 'No thank you.' Then they said, 'Why not?' Which really surprised me since I've built my life in such a way that very few people in it try to make me do things that I don't want to do. Present company excluded."

Another dig against Peter and one against me, Kate noted. *She should stop trying to pretend she's so nice and take a little responsibility for her hostility.*

"So I said, 'Because I don't want to,' and got annoyed until they sulked off into their car, leaving behind the buddy who worked overnight. I said to Pearl, 'Let's get out of here. When those guys come back drunk we're going to have big problems.' This was before the gay rights bill so they could have thrown us out too. But Pearl was stubborn, so we stayed. Still, I barricaded the door and propped up the back of a chair underneath the knob. Then I closed and secured all the windows."

The guy stretched out across the aisle was scratching his

head furiously and sliding his hands down his pants for comfort.

"That night we were sleeping and at five in the morning they tried to kick in the door. They climbed up the trellis and tried to climb in through the windows. And all along I thought, *we can't scream for help* because we were two naked women in one bed. So we lay there absolutely silent, holding each other's hands, and eventually they went away laughing. I know that the owner heard the commotion. I mean, they could hear Pearl's orgasms, surely they heard these guys trying to gang-rape us. But no one came to help. The next morning when we checked out the desk clerk didn't say a word."

Why is she always telling me these stories about how awful men are? Kate thought. *She's trying to make me feel guilty for having a man. She's manipulating me. I hate when she talks like this.*

"You'll see," Molly said, settling back down against her lover's shoulder. "Someday if we travel together, it's really different. Everywhere you go men come over and talk to you. They always interrupt. They always want your attention."

A couple of cops strode into the car in their blues, swinging sticks skillfully on their leather straps. Then they hit the sticks into their hands, the way girls on a softball team throw the ball into their own mitts. The slap is the thing.

"Move on," one cop said, hitting the guy on the wrapped bottoms of his feet.

"Where to?" the guy said, rolling over and closing his eyes.

"I'm coming back in ten minutes," the cop said. "Don't be here."

Then he and his partner sauntered out again. The guy took one last look and then rolled over and went back to sleep.

"If he's planning on hitting the soles of every sleeping person in the next car it's going to take him more than ten minutes to get back to this one," Molly whispered.

But Kate had other things on her mind.

"Molly, why don't you get yourself a second girlfriend? If you had a regular girlfriend you wouldn't be so dependent on me. You really want a lesbian and I'll never be a lesbian. I like cock."

"Do you have to keep saying that? Please stop saying that, it ruins my whole week."

Kate's teeth were set into her peach-colored lips. She wore no makeup. Her eyes were creased.

"What are you, some kind of martyr?"

"Good question."

"Well, if that's your trip, Molly, then take it somewhere else."

"Please don't say that. You're going to make me walk away from you and it's not even my stop."

"Don't play that hurt martyr game with me."

The sun was setting later and later, so the afternoons had begun to spread out luxuriously. As they walked along in silence from the station Kate noticed that it was really warm and people had all the time in the world. Soon it would be so hot that no one would have to wear jackets and people could sit up on the roofs talking about going to the country.

"Do you think I could have AIDS?"

"No," Molly said. "Can I come in?"

They were standing in front of Kate's building.

"Don't do that. You know you can't come in."

Peter was home and conspicuously busy. He was making dinner obviously. He was silent. He was moping. He was a martyr too but not even a cheerful one.

"Peter, just say what you have to say. This is not 'Million Dollar Movie.' Just say it."

"You should move in with her for a while." He spat it out. "Then she'll see how much I put up with."

She knew what he wanted. It was obvious. He wanted her to put her arms around him and console him but she couldn't do that. She was sick and tired of both of them.

"Look, Pete. Get this through your thick skull. I don't want to live with her. I want to live with you. Pete? Pete?"

"What?"

"You think the trouble we're having is because of her, but the truth is that it's about me. Me. I am changing. Do you understand?"

His face was flat.

"I'm changing, and do you know what? I'm glad. Do you want to be the same person with the same opinions and the same habits for the rest of your life? Give in, Pete."

"Everything's for you," he said. "You're selfish."

"I'm changing my life. Why don't you stop wishing I wouldn't and do something about yours?"

34

KATE

▲▲▲

She was of two minds about going out of town. Frankly, Kate
wanted to get away from her lovers, and she wanted to sit down
with the carpenter and work intensively on her project. But there
was also some nagging suspicion that this was the kind of moment best not left unattended and anything was capable of happening behind her back. So she had called Pearl the night before
to go over their agenda and realized, again, that she really did
need to go up there and see the wooden framing structure for
herself. She could not risk arriving at the library site on the
morning of the installation to find something wrong with the
frames.

It was a strange bus ride. Kate exhausted all her normal
traveling rituals with a speedy ambivalence. She ate her food
before Yankee Stadium, lifelessly leafed through and then dis-
missed her newspaper and once again carefully considered the
pros and cons of owning a Walkman. It came in handy at times

like these, but didn't one's sense of humanity demand striking up a conversation with one's neighbor instead of plugging into a square plastic box? Kate looked at the man sitting next to her. He was listening to his Walkman. When she closed her eyes and pressed back into her seat she could feel vaguely operatic vibrations emanating from his head and passing through the cushions.

Again she looked for distractions, but the bumpy road made reading or sketching impossible. Besides, there was a large, flat calm where her general anxiety really should have been, and then on top of it a tiny, nervous, constant throb.

But she did feel instinctively good about Pearl. That was one thing about Molly's friends. They were reliable and very cheap. Of course, men were helping too. After all it was Spiros who had gotten her the funding and he good-naturedly promised to organize champagne and hors d'oeuvres for the actual opening.

"Although I'm not a great believer in installations," he told her, "I am even more atheistic when it comes to sour grapes."

The bus ride had been interesting for the first thirty minutes when they passed through an extended Harlem that was a collection of churches, beauty parlors and liquor stores. It had main drags, it had decimated areas, it had music schools and a liberation bookstore. It had Jamaican meat patties and a good crust pie between the projects and luxury brownstones. It had everything a poor city had plus certain things that only Harlem had and it was black and Latin all over except around the edges and a few pockets of new white people moving in or old white people who had endured or brand-new Korean businesses. After Harlem there was nothing to look at for hours.

It was Thursday. On Tuesday night Justice had met for the first time in its new home. The membership had simply grown too large for anybody's basement. Now they gathered in the abandoned Saint Mark's bathhouse, closed down by the mayor right after he closed the Mineshaft. The crowd was huge, especially since Justice had been joined by Fury, the women-with-AIDS group. Now Daisy, an older Puerto Rican woman with long gray hair, co-facilitated the meetings with James. She began every session with a big smile on her face and an announcement.

△△△

"If there is anyone here from the Federal Bureau of Investigation or the New York City Police Department, you are required by law to identify yourself now."

Everyone would be silent for a moment and look around, then their faces would open into broad grins and they would get back to work. Defiance was Justice's bread and butter.

The presence of the Furies changed the Justice guys just a bit. It made for a coed institution, one in which, except for a few indiscretions, the sexes rarely mixed intimately.

"That puts us in a special category," Molly said after one particularly lively meeting, "with other famous fag/dyke teams like the Catholic Church, Hollywood and the Olympics."

The crowd filled the empty tile pool, sitting around the ledge and on the tasteful steps. The cubicles had been turned into nap rooms, not offices.

"This is a grass-roots movement," Daisy said. "We don't need offices. We are employed in offices. Steal Xerox, take White-Out, use postage machines, make phone calls. Your job is a prison of measured time. So make their time work for you."

The baths had seemed musty to Kate at first, but the men oohed and aahed, remembering what it was like *before*, remembering with some nervousness the last time each of them had been there. They were warm and joking with one another, like adults returning to the sandlot.

"I feel like Judas Maccabaeus returning to the trashed-out temple," Bob said. He clapped his long, sleek hands together and reached up to the cobwebbed archway. "Oh Lord, let those glory days be with us once again. Oh unknown dick, oh joy, oh most angelic thought."

Throughout the meeting different people's wristwatch alarms kept going off with little beeps.

"What's going on?" Kate asked. "Is everyone schedule-crazy? Whenever I come to these meetings watch alarms keep going off."

"It's to remind them to take their AZT," Molly told her. "Every four hours."

"Oh."

Fabian took up his old spot in the corner and tried out his old pose, an imaginary drink in hand and his left foot flat back against a marble pillar.

"You know what comes to mind right away?" Fabian said.

"What?" Kate asked curiously as he twisted the leather thong hanging from his belt.

"The Village People singing 'Macho Man.' Remember that one?"

"Not really," Kate said. "I've never listened to the radio much."

"Disco, disco," Bob said. "If ever I foresake thee."

No one had given them permission to use the old bathhouse. They just took it. Justice was getting very aggressive. They had no ideology except stopping AIDS, and because they had made that their priority, they behaved as though it was the world's priority.

"Are you upset about this?" James asked commuters when Justice stopped traffic on the George Washington Bridge. "You should be as upset about AIDS."

Attendance at meetings had grown to well over five hundred and numbers like that meant all kinds, all kinds. There were the tough street Furies who had all been around the block a couple of times. There were distinguished homosexuals with white-boy jobs, who had forgotten that they were queer until AIDS came along and everyone else reminded them. At first the white collars had wanted to bring lawsuits and carry out polite picket lines, while the Furies had been willing to bash in a few heads at the expense of getting bashed themselves. But soon the two factions were able to unite in anger and a commitment to direct action when the homos found out what a lifetime of anger could create and the Furies discovered that nothing raises the level of outrage as efficiently as the level of expectation.

"Imagining what they deserve and then fighting for it," said Bob, "is something that anyone with nothing to lose can easily learn, if they have a determined personality."

There was also a contingent of old-time radicals of various stripes who had rioted in the sixties at Stonewall, in Newark, with the Young Lords, with SDS, and hadn't done a goddamn thing since. No straight men showed up at all.

"Straight men don't know how to take care of other people," Daisy explained. "And they don't work well in groups."

There was a band of veterans from the now defunct women's liberation movement who were the only ones who had been consistently politically active for the last decade, and so knew better than anyone else how to make flyers, how to do phone trees, the quickest way to wheat-paste, and who weren't afraid of getting arrested.

"Being a woman in Justice means being in leadership," Daisy once said. "As soon as you walk in the room all the guys turn around and say, 'Now what?'"

"We like dykes," the guys would chant every once in a while when the women did something really great. And there were lots and lots of handsome young men who intended to live to be handsome old men or even just aging queens. They were the organization's best recruitment force, since Justice's favorite activity after raising hell was the boyfriend parade.

The man sitting next to Kate on the bus finished listening to his cassettes. After one awkward exchanged glance, he took out a copy of the *New York Native* and opened it directly to the personals.

"I love that part of the paper," she said, peering over his shoulder. "Especially all the little codes. Like *c/b/t*. That means cock and ball torture, right?"

"Excuse me?"

He wasn't embarrassed at all. He was more curious and amused.

"You know what interests me most?" she said. "When they specify *uncut*. Who would have thought that foreskin was the necessary component to constructing the man of your dreams."

"Well," he said, looking down his glasses, "the straight ones are far more insidious. Have you checked the back of the *New York Review of Books* lately? You know, 'Distinguished professional gentleman into domination and Schopenhauer, looking for blond female sixteen to eighteen for permanent relationship.'"

"I'm not defending heterosexuality at all," Kate said, sending her blue eyes directly into his brown ones. She leaned over when she said that and rested her chin on the top of her fist. Then he had to take her seriously because there was something so proper and bizarre about her at the same time. She knew he saw the suit. He saw the big black shoes with white socks and the thick, black glasses.

"Are you gay?" he asked smiling.

She didn't know what to say.

"Maybe."

"Well," he said, playing along. "Have you ever been gay?"

"Oh yes," she said. "By the way, is gay something you *are* or does it depend on who you're in bed with at that precise moment?"

"It depends on whose love helps you grow the most and is most comforting to you given a state of nature."

"This isn't that social-construction-versus-essentialist argument that I've heard so much about, is it?"

"No," he said. "It means, try thinking back to a woman you loved and never touched and then figure out why not."

"What are you, a therapist?"

"No," he said. "I'm just one of those people you meet on a bus ride somewhere who you will never see again, but who asks you memorable questions."

They laughed together and then each looked away at something else for a while. Then they both turned back.

"I fell in love with an actress in the last play I worked on, before I left the theater. *The Blacks* by Jean Genet. Do you know it?"

"Of course."

The bus rolled on. What had been jolting only minutes before was suddenly a smooth and comforting lull.

"I was ready to quit the whole scene, but as one last gesture I jumped at the chance to be Sandra's dresser for the first few weeks of the run. You have to be calm to be the dresser. You catch the actress in her most vulnerable moment, coming off one emotion and preparing for the other. You have to be so smooth and silent that you are one with her or just air. You undress her. You see her nude. You cover her up again. She doesn't look at you. She is deep in thought. One second later she belongs to everyone but right then she belongs only to you."

Kate could smell Sandra King's body right there on the bus, just the way she used to do every night zipping her dress up over those soft, brown breasts.

"One night we kissed. I'd actually forgotten until this very moment that we had kissed. But we did. Thinking back on it she was probably gay. It was harder to tell in those days. In fact, I'm sure of it. She was married but that never means anything. Peter put the make on her, she told me. But she wasn't interested. She brushed him off over coffee."

"Who's Peter?"

"My husband."

"Oh, now I see."

He smiled again, very warmly.

"Peter always wants to be close to the women I'm attracted to. It's a way of appropriating my experiences. But she wasn't interested in him at all. Not at all."

"Or in you."

"That too."

"My favorite thing about being gay," said the man on the bus, "is that there is something so starkly honest about it and so involved with people's secret lives. I can be what straight people only imagine." He played with the gold band on his right hand. "My lover is waiting for me in Kingston. Is that where you're going? Maybe we can give you a lift."

"I have to change for another bus. But, thank you."

"Well," he said, folding the paper under his arm. "We are, after all, members of the same church. Very few heterosexual women know about c/b/t. If I'd thought you were really straight I would have said that my *roommate* is meeting me in Kingston."

"I love men too," she said, feeling much older than him.

"Oh yes," he said, shifting his body away from hers, still smiling, but with less conviction. From then on it was pure artifice. They chatted a bit about books, then movies, but the moment between them had dissolved.

It was our gayness that connected us, she realized later. Not our love of men. It is the danger that brings you together, makes you need each other and feel so close.

35
KATE

△△

Kate leaned against the wall of the small bus station next to the water fountain. She could see everything from that spot: who went into the bathroom and how long it took them to come out. She could tell who was smoking cigarettes and who was smoking pot. She could hear every telephone conversation.

Kate picked the chocolate coating off a candy bar with her teeth. It suddenly flashed in her mind that her relationship with Peter might not last forever. Her response was a tiny terror. She lost her cool. It had snuck up on her like a shadow, without any premeditation, and then passed with no imaginable picture.

One drizzling night she and Peter had come out of the subway and she'd spotted Molly walking ahead of them on the other side of the street.

"I think he meant *space-aged* in the Baudrillard sense of the word," Peter was saying. "As generically modern and technological, not exclusively pertaining to rocket ships, although not completely independent of it either."

Molly had looked so solid. Her shoulders were squared and she looked tough, completely in charge. It was late and dark but she didn't rush with fear, just kept on steadily from an internal power that compensated for size and caste. Kate had watched herself with Peter. They were loud and obvious. They moved all over the sidewalk and said anything they liked. At the same time Molly was aware of every presence and event in her path and made herself invisible to all of it. She was quiet, like one of the buildings. She was a shadow on a wet street.

"Operator," said a balding man in a light blue suit, "I'd like to charge this to my company's calling card."

Kate took a sip of water.

"I'd like to charge this to calling card 212-555-9814-3051." Kate said it again to herself: "212-555-9814-3051."

She said it one more time as she walked slowly into the ladies' room and scrawled it on a piece of toilet tissue.

It was at a recent meeting that James and Daisy had asked for credit card numbers. Justice divided up into search committees to make the collection more systematic. There was a whole caucus of waiters working in expensive restaurants who could save the carbons from processed charge card forms. There were lovers of the dead and dying and the dying themselves who hadn't gotten around to canceling their plastic. There were the sick but still surviving who promised to fill out all the forms being passed around the room. And there was a battalion of travelers who volunteered to hang out around pay phones in airports with open ears.

"Let AT&T pay for the phone revolution," Daisy said.

"Transatlantic phone sex?" asked Fabian, who considered it his personal responsibility to ensure that every Justice project was sex-affirmative.

Kate waited for the guy in the blue suit to disappear, then she dialed the operator.

"I'd like to charge this to my company's calling card," she said. Her skin was tingling. She had never done anything like this before. Peter and Kate had often prided themselves on how radical they were. They were artists, after all, and not stock-brokers. They'd never been rich, although they weren't working shit jobs either, but they'd never had children or bought a co-op. Their lifestyle was their politics in action. But, standing in a sea-foam-green bus station in rural New York, that all seemed rather superficial. She realized, waiting for the operator to complete the call, that there was something repulsive at the base of this kind of thinking.

"We have fundamentally different values," Molly had told her one day.

"Because you hate men and I see their humanity?" Kate answered.

"That's not exactly how I would put it."

"Well," Kate said sometime later in that conversation, "I don't think we're as far apart as you say. I mean, when the shit comes down, we'll both be on the same side of the barricades."

"The shit is already down."

"I mean when people are dying in the streets."

"Kate, people are dying in the streets. It's not the movies, where the world divides into freedom fighters and brownshirts. Here in New York City there are people who take action and people who do nothing. Doing nothing is a position. It means giving approval without having to actively say so."

"212," Kate said into the phone: "212-555-9814-3051."

It took only a minute, it was so easy.

"Hello?"

"Hello, Scottie? This is Kate. I didn't expect you to answer the phone."

"Yeah, I got out early."

It was the third time Scott had been in Sinai since the beginning of spring. It wasn't his skin this month. This month it was pneumocystis. She had been prepared that time, walking into the hospital room to see silvery blue oxygen tubes going into his nose.

"Scott?"

"Yes."

"212-555-9814-3051."

"Great," he said. "That's the seventieth number we've gotten in. The phone codes are beating out Diners Club four to one. Will you be back on Monday? That's credit card mobilization day."

"I think so. Scott?"

"Yes?"

"Sometimes a person has to stop talking about art for a moment and take a look around."

"I know," he said. "I know exactly what you mean."

△△△

36
PETER

△△△

There was a man on Second Avenue wearing a sign that said I Hate Jesus Christ. Whenever someone walked by he would tell them, "I accept Jesus Christ as my personal enemy. I have been badly hurt by Christianity this year. This has not been a good year for me and the Christians."

Then there were the guys on the corner selling raffles to "help stop drug abuse." Peter wanted to stop drug abuse but he couldn't be sure that this was the most effective way. So he had to say no. Then the kids selling got really frustrated and screamed out after him, "What's the matter, you like drug abuse?" So he knew immediately that he had made the right decision.

Peter was glad that Kate was out of his hair for a few days. She was really annoying him. If she wanted more independence, let her have it. He felt like having a few days in Manhattan on his own. He felt like a sailor. He could go anywhere he wanted and do anything he wanted and no one would know that he had done it.

The first thing that happened was that he talked much less. Whenever he was in the house he had no one to talk to, so he tried to think about intellectual things, about art matters, but there was no one to talk them over with, so he ended up thinking about what he was feeling because there was no way to avoid it. There was no distraction. That's when he started feeling like he wanted revenge.

He ate in restaurants because it was easier and that way nothing had to be planned. During meals he would talk to the waiter or the guy sitting next to him at the counter. He watched TV. He made phone calls to old friends and to his brother, who was teaching math in Ann Arbor. He went running for hours.

Initially Peter's goal was Central Park, but something led him off the track. Officially it may have been the late-June hordes of tourists lining the avenues or the heat or too much car exhaust. But when he found himself deciding to take a rest, just about the time he arrived in front of Ronald Horne's Castle, he had returned to the scene of the crime. This is where Kate had really betrayed him. This was the lobby where she joined the other side. He sat down on an alligator-skin sofa. This is where she had humiliated him on television by pretending to be gay.

He slid in behind the rhino-skin bar and read over the menu. Each drink was called the colonial name of a contemporary country. There was the Ceylon Sling, the Indochina Surprise, the Rhodesia Twist. He ordered a Gold Coast: banana, pineapple, rum and oil decorated with a replica of a sacred religious icon on the end of a toothpick. He was about to order a Bay of Pigs Pâté when right in front of him, crossing the room like he owned it, which he did, was Ronald Horne, head landlord of the world. He had that look that celebrities have, like they're on television even when they're standing in front of you because their makeup is always perfect and they always seem to be correctly lit, not to mention well fed.

He still has all his hair, Peter noticed with a slight twinge of admiration. Horne was headed straight for the door marked Bwana.

I've got to follow him, Peter thought, leaping from his seat with the determination of a man on a mission. *I've got to see what his dick looks like.*

"Wait a minute, buddy," said a huge goon in a loincloth and war paint. "The boss is in there."

"I know," Peter said clutching his drink. "But I've got to go too."

"No one watches Horne piss," said the faithful savage in his South Brooklyn accent. "Those balls are worth their weight in gold. In fact, they're worth a hundred times their weight in gold."

"But urine is urine," said Peter.

"Look, fella, I got my orders. Now why don't you let a slave girl fan you with a peacock feather for a few minutes and wait your turn."

Peter was mad. This was where his wife stabbed him in the back. He wasn't going to be pushed around by some strong-arm in a gold lamé jockstrap.

"You listen to me," he said, waving around the toothpick so that its replica shrunken head kept just missing the guard's oft broken nose. "You've got a morally dubious job here, do you realize that? Why don't you go into something more fun like repossessing family farms?"

That made him feel good. That made him feel real good.

"Get the fuck out of here, right now," Goliath said, and before Peter had a chance to think it over, he was back on the hot sidewalk feeling better, better and stronger than he had in a long time. He had made his stand. He'd shown Kate and he'd shown that little bitch too.

Peter jogged home triumphant. He worked out at the gym. He ran errands. He went to the hardware store. He went to the shoe repair. He went to the Xerox store across the street from the bowling alley.

"Hi," she said.

"Hi," he said. "Do I know you?"

"We met bowling. Remember? I had a copy of *Mourning Becomes Electra*."

Oh thank God, thought Peter. He could have gotten down on his knees and reached up from his heart to heaven. *Thank you for bringing this woman to me.*

When Shelley agreed to go have a cup of coffee after work, he knew how much he really needed this. And he knew that he could really like her too. She was beautiful and New York sexy, ethnic. He could learn to love her. She would grow up soon. She'd be terrific at thirty.

"Do you want to go to heaven?" he asked, sitting across the table.

"No," she said.

"You mean to tell me that when you die you don't want to go to heaven?"

"Oh, when I die, yeah. I thought you were going now."

She's smart, he thought. *She's funny.*

When they made love for the first time that day it wasn't passionate love. It was cool. But he knew the passion would come. There was already an immediate tenderness and easy familiarity. Shelley pulled at his penis like it was a fun new toy. He loved when women played with his dick. Engagement or absentmindedness were both sexy in their own ways.

"It always surprises me how big balls are," she said. "The way that everyone talks about pricks all the time you'd never know that balls were anything in this world. Except for gay men. They like balls. They call them 'baskets' or maybe that's with a dick too, but they like them 'low-slung.' "

"How do you know?" he said, worried for a minute. "You're not gay, are you? You're not bi or unsure or in transition? You're heterosexual, right? You choose cock."

"Don't worry," she said, a little unnerved. "My brother is gay. We talk about that stuff all the time."

"Well, I need a break from it," he said, taking her in his arms. "So let's not talk about it when we're together, okay?"

"Sure," she said and then she thought it over a bit. "Sure, why not?"

She had just dropped out of her senior year at NYU which

made her plenty young. Young enough that Peter didn't even ask.

Later she asked him, "What makes a man a good lover?"

And he said, "Take your time. Make sure she gets enough clit. Touch everything."

Who was the person he had become that afternoon? Peter had never seen himself so romantic and funny. Well, not never, of course, but seriously not for a long, long time.

They walked out together that night, along the edge of China-town where they could smell the bok choy cooking out of every window. They could smell the leftover fish in the garbage and see people taking an easy smoke for the first time all day. Peter had a new woman's hand in his and it was softer, warmer and a completely different shape.

There was a cop car parked on Canal and Mott. There's always a lot more crime in the summer, people get sweaty and crowded together. They get bored and want new things in their lives. They get angry very fast.

"Let's check it out," Shelley said, so they joined the pack watching from stoops and street corners, leaning on doorframes and the trunk of the patrol car.

"If you look at the light," he told her, "you can't see the light. You have to look at its effect on objects. The whirling white and red on top of a police car is meaningless without the faces it stripes. Without them it is only an appliance. We have to explore each object beyond its functional identity."

She hooked her fingers in the back belt loop of his pants.

"You know, Peter," she said, rubbing her palm against his stomach as they stood watching, "it must be very lonely for you because you think you're the only one watching. But that's not true. I'm watching you, Peter. I see you."

Has any man ever been that happy?

37
MOLLY

△△△

Thursday night after work Molly stopped by Daisy's place with a six-pack plus a couple of extra beers. The double feature that day had been *Persona* and *Cries and Whispers*, two proto-lesbian classics, but one really had to be in the mood.

On the way over, she ran into Charlie who was, as usual, looking hungry and wanting to get high. Usually getting high was the priority, but every once in a while he had to take time out from selling nickel bags on the corner so that he could quickly eat.

"I don't mind feeding him," Molly had told Kate once. "Because everyone needs to eat."

But that did not erase the fact that he brought in three times as much money a week as she did, but still managed to be homeless because it all went to drugs. That's why she got pissed off when, once in a blue moon, he would try to guilt-trip her for having a home when he didn't. She also knew that while drug addicts are real people in that they get hungry and cold and sick and die, there is a big hunk missing from them somehow. And for that reason, they couldn't be treated as fully human because they would just rip you off and exploit you every chance they got. But this time Charlie was hungry enough to want to eat, so Molly sat down with him at the counter at Jeanette's Polish Home Cooking. She felt like talking for a minute anyway, and could not trust him to not pocket the waitress's tip.

The fact was after all these apprehensions that Charlie was really okay and if drugs hadn't taken over his entire life, they could have stayed friends.

"I'm telling you, Molly," he said, wolfing down a chicken cutlet with two vegetables, "this country is filled with wasted potential. You got those white boys running everything and it's so built-in they don't even know that they're running it. I don't mean the big boys I mean your regular white man on the street. Lets face it, I could sit in the White House smoking coke all day long and I would still be a better vice president than you-know-who. But there are revolutionary possibilities out there. As soon as people get their priorities together then we'll see some radical action."

Molly hated when Charlie ran this rap. He'd be an armchair radical if he had an armchair.

"Charlie, your only priority is cocaine. Don't give me this *revolutionary* bullshit."

She felt bad the minute she'd said it, though, because he looked humiliated, which made her acknowledge that they weren't equals since he was dependent on her for food. Therefore he couldn't tell her to go fuck herself because he wanted to eat. So she just paid the check and split.

At Daisy's everyone was sitting around the table doing a mailing of the People with AIDS newsletter. They were humming and chatting. The radio was blasting pretty loud from the salsa station, so feet were tapping and bodies were alternately moving and tightly bent over piles of envelopes. They folded, stuffed and stamped sheets of newsprint that might save some lives and would definitely increase the quality of others.

First there was Daisy, a combination aging Latin hippie and

librarian. She was one of those people who always had really interesting information and had a hard time letting other people have interesting information too. Still, she was great in front of a room where it was a one-way thing. Daisy wore bifocals on a black string around her neck and had gray hair that had never been cut. She was what is known as a "neighborhood person." She knew every single face on the block, what they needed and whether she could help them find it or not.

Then there was her lover, Trudy, who used to be a cop. Trudy knew all the laws to the letter and so, whenever there was a demonstration planned, she was in charge of "cop-duty." That meant keeping an eye on the boys and girls in blue at all times and recording all the infractions they couldn't keep themselves from committing.

"Give me a break, sweetheart," some cop would inevitably say. "That's the fourth time you've written down my badge number in the last half hour."

"I have to write it down every time you do something illegal," she would answer. "If you don't want it written down then don't move."

She drove them crazy every chance she got. They couldn't get away with the male cops searching female arrestees. They couldn't get away with stopping picket lines.

"Picket lines are legal as long as they keep moving," she'd yell out, opening her little blue memo pad. "And you know it."

"Cops," she'd sigh every now and then. "What a bunch of punks."

Then there was a really quiet girl with black black hair and a devilish grin. That was Sam, Trudy's sister, who had just hitchhiked back from Oklahoma. She wore a powder blue cowboy shirt and one of those string ties with a silver Navaho tie clip. They called her Sam because she looked exactly like Sam Shepard. Her real name was Dorothy. Sam didn't say much, she drank slow and folded and stuffed and sealed envelopes all night long. Trudy didn't drink anything but seltzer but she didn't mind being around the more indulgent.

"I like the smell of beer," she said. "I'll never deny that."

The house was small and comfortable with a lot of plastic plus old-fashioned things. There was a big old-time TV that sat in a wooden box with legs and on top was a rosary that was clearly in use. There were two big Santería candles and a photograph of Lolita Lebrón.

"I've got all the angles covered," she said.

Daisy had shot drugs for a couple of years, quit for ten and then went back after a bad breakup. It was only for a few months the second time around but she'd picked the wrong months. When all the reports started coming into the library where she worked, Daisy ran out and got tested first thing, so she knew she was positive and started watching the symptoms appear. Trudy had heard through some gay friends that doctors at a couple of hospitals were testing experimental drugs on AIDS patients. Daisy was reading everything she could get her hands on and got interested in a drug called Ampligen which seemed to work as well as the AZT but didn't have the side effects. It didn't make you nauseated and it didn't give you diarrhea. But the hospital turned her down on a formality: she was a woman.

"I demanded an explanation," she said, telling the story for the fourteen hundredth time. "I went after the doctors. I called them at work. I called them at home. I started going out and sitting on their front lawns in Great Neck. Why weren't women allowed to take Ampligen? Finally, one guy, maybe from Saint Luke's, got so sick of me that he shouted out of the window of the commuter train, 'It's the company. Blame the company.' So, I started going after them. As we say in Justice, What did I have to lose?"

Sam decided to go out for more beer, since she'd already heard that story once that day. Each woman put two dollars into her white Stetson hat.

"By that time I'd found the other women who wanted to try Ampligen too. But believe me, pharmaceutical companies are harder to get through to than doctors. But I haven't been a librarian on the Lower East Side for fifteen years for nothing. I know how to get information despite their iron bitch receptionists and their bosses with Aqua Velva accents who sound like they're standing on a golf course no matter what lies they're spouting. You can just picture the plaid slacks. So, we got on the Amtrak and went down to meet them in person."

Trudy got up to turn down the radio and then stood behind Daisy with her arms around her neck, pressing her breasts against Daisy's back.

"The cops tried to haul us away of course, but fortunately Trudy was there with her rule book."

Daisy reached out lovingly behind and brought Trudy's face to hers so they were cheek to cheek.

"Finally we got the official explanation. *Birth defects.* They won't give dying women treatment because they're afraid of being brought to court on birth defects. I mean, I understand protecting a fetus, I was raised Catholic after all, but a woman has to live too. So, I told the guy that first of all, two of us were gay and secondly the other one had no intention of getting pregnant. She has AIDS, for God's sake."

"What did he say?" Molly asked, noticing Sam sliding back into the apartment with a six-pack in a brown bag and some kind of pint in a smaller one.

"He says, 'Who's going to protect my company against lawsuits? That's what I want to know.' So I got in touch with Justice. James helped me set up a contact sheet of a hundred and fifty women with AIDS around the country who are interested in Ampligen and don't plan on getting pregnant, or who are willing to have an abortion in case they do get pregnant, which can happen, after all."

"So, are you taking Ampligen?"

Sam opened a beer for Daisy and Molly and one beer for herself and a seltzer for Trudy. Then she took a taste out of a small bottle of Wild Turkey and left it open on the table for anyone else who desired.

"Not yet. They claim they're going to start a protocol for women soon, but they say they're going to run it in Pittsburgh. There are at least four thousand women with AIDS in this country and most of them are right here in New York City and most are too poor or too disorganized to get down to fucking Pittsburgh so there's still a lot of work to do on this, but we'll do it," she said.

Then Trudy turned up the radio.

38

MOLLY

ΔΔΔΔΔΔΔΔΔΔΔΔΔΔΔΔΔΔΔΔΔΔΔΔΔΔΔΔΔΔΔΔΔΔΔΔΔΔΔΔΔΔΔΔΔΔΔΔΔΔΔΔΔΔΔΔΔΔΔΔΔΔΔΔΔΔΔΔΔΔΔΔΔΔ

"So, do you live in Oklahoma?"

"No, I live right here. A few blocks over. I was just in Oklahoma for vacation."

"I never really thought of it as a tourist spot," Molly said. The street was wet because it had been raining, which meant that all the headlights reflected off the asphalt and there was a special sound from the tires on the water.

"Sometimes I need to go somewhere else," Sam said as they walked along. "Sometimes it's desert or just flat."

At one point that evening, right after the last envelope had been stuffed and stamped, Molly and Trudy and Sam had gone into the bathroom to smoke cigarettes because Daisy felt that a sick woman should not have to put up with cigarette smoke wafting through her apartment. Normally Molly didn't smoke, but after all that beer, she just felt like it. She just felt like being a normal New Yorker with no pretensions. The lamp was busted though, so the three of them sat there in the dark; Trudy on the toilet and Sam and Molly on the bathtub's edge, passing the red ember back and forth, the way that girls like to take hits off the same cigarette. It was quiet and delicious and made each one of them want to sit in the black bathroom longer than was socially acceptable. Halfway to the filter Sam put her hand around Molly's waist and then held it there, steady.

When they returned to the lit room again Molly and Sam had a secret which they reinforced by never looking each other in the eye, as though there were absolutely nothing going on. Molly realized that Sam was a good liar and a smooth operator and a real drinker with a few secrets.

So, they both left Daisy's at the same time and walked in the same direction. Molly was a little drunk and couldn't understand everything Sam said but at one point she definitely heard "baby doll" and Sam was probably referring to her. Finally Sam kissed her; she was all tongue. Then she put her arm around Molly and protected her from men on the street who said stupid insulting things to them all the way to Sam's house.

Molly hadn't fully comprehended who this woman was until they got to her apartment. It was a fifties dime-store novel about a pregentrification bohemia that no one could live in anymore because of high rents and lack of inclination. Sam led her up rickety stairs past a front door with a busted lock, past the beat-up mailboxes hanging open on mangled hinges. Everyone in the building was Chinese. The hallways were decorated with red hanging things left over from the New Year and all the apartment doors were open so they could see old-world grandmothers in quilted jackets and white T-shirts cooking rice on hot plates. There were lots of beds in each room and walls papered with magazine covers, calendar pages and red fringe. Tired men shuffled to bathrooms in the hall, barefoot on the torn linoleum.

It was one room. It was spare. There was no refrigerator. Her beer was sitting on the windowsill trying to keep cool in the June rain. There was a bulb from the ceiling, a bed she had built, a TV.

"Hungry?"

There were no chairs. There was an ancient stove. Some collector could make it into a planter for a small tree in a large space. The window faced a wall, so there was no breeze and no light. Sam pulled off the griddle and cooked over an open flame. She cooked up something poor like millet and cabbage, standing there sweating in her T-shirt, muscles traveling under her skin, being quiet.

The TV was on. Molly sat on the floor and watched the TV but on the side of her vision was this woman cooking it up. There were probably a thousand stars they couldn't see and then Sam brought her a plateful. It felt so good.

"No one ever cooks for me."

It was private. There was no talking. There was a sound from the TV but it was benign and there was a woman, moving, bringing her something hot.

Sam wore a T-shirt instead of a bra. She had thighs of steel. She pressed her thumbs inside Molly, not like those girls who think their hands are substitute penises. She had technique. When Molly ate her Sam leaned back on her knees as far as she could go. She knew how to accept pleasure. Her clit swelled in Molly's hand like a huge, undulating sea urchin. They lay on the floor. Her hands were big and rough. She was a Girl of the Golden West. She was a memory from another time.

"I can fix anything," she said. "I can drive any vehicle. I can pick up any instrument. I like to go out in the woods. You see lines on the ground, but they are not lines. They are shadows from the trees."

"You're so sexy to me," Molly said. "You're a cowgirl."

Later Sam was very tender. Molly could see the headlights moving against the wall outside the window as cars turned corners on their way to various places.

"Do you have a girlfriend?" Sam asked.

"Yeah, but she's married."

"What's her husband like?"

"Large and blobby, like most big men when they get old. Clean-cut, boring. You could trust him for directions on the subway but wouldn't want to talk to him about anything beyond that. If Peter and I were strangers at the same party, we would never get around to meeting each other."

"What's she like?"

"I love her."

"How do lesbians keep from giving each other AIDS?" Sam asked, stroking everything.

"Don't eat her when she has her period if you're not sure. That's all. It's easy. Do you think you might have AIDS?"

"No," Sam said. "I used to live with someone who had it though."

"Did you have sex?"

"No."

"Share needles?"

Sam nodded.

"Be careful then."

"I'd really like some coffee and pie," Sam said.

"What's out there at three o'clock on Friday morning?"

They ran down the list. There were chicken tostadas. There were late after-hours places, Puerto Rican social clubs and black-leather rich artists' bars. There were always twenty-four-hour Korean markets but no coffee and pie this side of the Hudson River that time of night.

"What about the Kiev?"

"No, I want the real thing, not that canned filling stuff," Sam said. "Let's just lie here and talk about pie."

Molly admired Sam's hands, which were cracked and swollen from working so hard in so many strange places. She ignored the tracks.

"Well," Molly said. "There's three-berry pie at Café Yaffa. There's Danish apple torte at Hiro's. There's pear-cranberry at Orlin. There's brandy walnut—"

"That's yuppie food," Sam said. "I want strawberry-rhubarb. The kind they sell in truck stops once you get out of Ohio. The kind you can always order anywhere in America and know it's going to be good."

"Is it still like that out there in America?" Molly asked. "I haven't been in so long it's hard to know."

"Somewhere out there is strawberry-rhubarb pie," Sam said. "And I want a piece."

In the morning Sam made them both coffee and then she turned on the TV.

"I like to watch TV in the morning," she said. "What's on?"

She pulled out a crinkled Sunday section from under the bed and started reading it with great seriousness.

"Oh, this looks good. 'Senator's daughter gets kidnapped. With Linda Blair.'"

"Can I tell you something?" Molly said, feeling like she was going to cry. Feeling so sad. "I have been waiting for two years to sit with my lover around a table with her friends and family, like I sat with you at Daisy's. For two years I have not been able to sleep in my lover's bed and say what I feel like saying or linger in the morning with someone to hold on to or watch TV with. Thank you."

"I'll be thinking of you," Sam said.

39

KATE

Pearl drove up in her truck and opened the door.

"Welcome to the country."

The truck made too much noise, so they rode together in a kind of friendly, necessary silence accompanied by mechanical squeals and groans, like an old mule hauling them up these American hills. There are not too many places left with mountainsides and here and there between the corn, a horse, a white one that looks right at you in your passing car and flares its nostrils.

"Oh, no, I'm thinking like a postcard," Kate yelled.

"That's what happens," Pearl answered. "Or some pastoral movie. I could turn on the radio for soundtrack. The only stations we get up here are country music or God."

"That's okay," Kate shouted over the rattling motor. "I'm happy."

They decided to go back to Pearl's place and relax, then

spend the whole next day working on the frames. The first thing that popped into Kate's head once they were quiet again was the classic city-dweller reaction to hitting the hills. *I've got to be out of my mind to live in New York.* She spent the next fifteen minutes in preliminary deliberation about moving. The fantasy, however, then shifted from images of peace of mind to those of hauling wood in the winter and sitting alone inside for weeks at a time, always eating her own cooking. Not being able to get books. It began to sound better as a summer home instead. Some old ramshackle farmhouse that would just need a little work. Then they could get out of the heat on the weekends. But that, after all, would mean buying a car and spending the next decade working on the house. So the house would become the center of your life, because nothing else substantial could be undertaken until it was finished. By this point in that line of thinking, Kate accepted that she was just visiting and relaxed a whole other layer into the well-worn front seat of Pearl's truck. The sun then set in a fiery red uranium sky.

"Look behind you on the next curve," Pearl shouted over the claptrap engine. "It's an optical illusion. It looks like the mountain is coming out of the lake but they're actually miles apart."

"You think you're almost there but you never arrive," Kate said, too quietly to be heard. And then louder, "Well, it's nice to know that illusion is not a human invention. It's something we have inherited from the natural world."

By the time they got to the house it was darker and summer, a summer night rich and luxurious. A window that led out to the garden was open and dark moths fluttered about the lamp.

"I've got the crew all organized," Pearl said. "We'll put the piece in and you can arrive in the afternoon, relaxed, with a glass of champagne. The park behind the library is the perfect location for a big installation like *People in Trouble*. You're lucky that the private sector is picking up the bill. How did you pull this off anyway?"

"Spiros, my art dealer, did it. He's one of those people who pulls strings and spares you the details. That way I don't have to think about logistics all the time."

"So you can reap the benefits and remain morally pure at the same time. We all need someone to do that for us."

"Yes."

Oh no, Kate thought. *Not another one of these moralists.*

"Well, anyway," Pearl said. "I'm excited about the project. We'll mount it in a straight line, about three-quarters of a city block long, beginning at Sixth Avenue and ending right at the foot of the stage. Then people can begin at the front of the piece and walk a long straight line until they've seen the whole thing, which will lead them right to Horne's feet."

"Horne?"

"Yeah, Horne, he's making the dedication of the new building, didn't you know?"

"No."

"It was on the front page of the Arts and Leisure section last Sunday."

"Oh, I didn't see it."

"Well, anyway," Pearl continued, "it will be one long viewing walk."

"No, run."

"Run?"

"Yes, Pearl, you don't walk through this piece. You run. You start at one end and run turning your head to the mural so that the images fly by quickly as though it were a movie, only there's no technology."

Pearl was quiet long enough for the topic to change.

"My lover, Becky, will be over soon," she said, rising. "Would you like some wine? Do you want to talk anymore about the piece?"

That smile again.

"No, tomorrow we'll go through everything and yes, I'd love some wine. Can we put on music? Do you have any opera? I'm in the mood for something fabulous and huge."

They sat back again, listening to *Tosca.* There was nothing outside, no motion. There was a sound, which was Callas, and there was another sound which had to do with the movement of glass and then the human throat.

Pearl was knitting, of all things. Kate guessed it was one of those habits a person acquired in the country when loneliness became unbearable. Was Pearl lonely? She seemed fine. Kate sank into her chair and closed her eyes. She didn't like being alone for more than three days, that she knew from experience. Three days was fine but then she needed a familiar body next to hers. Whose? Peter's or Molly's. Either one would do.

"How do you feel?" Pearl asked, looking up.

"I don't know," Kate answered without thinking. Then she considered the question privately. She had no idea. There was a dullness, a soreness, a large blank. "There's a wall somewhere in my chest and I guess it needs to be broken down but I don't know why exactly or even what it is. There's this solid heavy thing I carry around with me. Sometimes I forget I even have it."

"Well, what's going to happen with you and Molly? With you and your husband?"

"I'm going to keep it like this for as long as I can."

"How do they feel about that?"

"They both hate me for it. Neither one will ever forgive me. Peter will bury it somewhere and Molly will wear it as a festering wound. I could never choose Molly. She has been most dramatically wronged, so I would have to spend years begging forgiveness and being extra kind. Besides, you know I could never leave Peter."

"Why not?"

"Habit."

"But do you love him?"

"Of course I do." Kate felt a horrible anxiety, like she was trying to breathe with her head under water. "I have great affection for him."

Her words resonated in the small cabin.

"Listen, Pearl, I don't want to live in a ghetto like lesbians do. I like men. I want to be universal. I want to be part of them."

Pearl's needles clicked in the yellow lamplight.

"I once tried to go back to men after I had been really hurt," Pearl said. "It was very . . . confusing."

"In what way exactly?"

"I felt absurd. I was inadequate from too much knowledge.

Playing the role only works if you don't know it's a role. You have to believe that that's the way it is."

"I like fucking. I like men. I'm not gay like the rest of you."

"Whoa," Pearl said. "Do you tell your husband and straight friends, 'I'm not straight like the rest of you'?" Pearl started to say something else but took a drink of wine instead. Then she said something entirely different. "Are you cold?"

She turned the record over. Then she started rolling a cigarette that she should have started rolling a long time before.

"I'm not gay," Kate said.

"I didn't say you were," Pearl answered, lighting it slowly with a wooden match.

"You implied it."

"Actually I don't think you're gay at all. Have some more wine. The night is a dark, dark well. We have music and comfortable chairs. We're very lucky."

"Can I use the phone?" Kate asked. There was an urgency in her voice. There was masked panic.

"Sure. It's in the kitchen." Pearl smoked very slowly.

Kate dialed home. There was no answer. She dialed Molly. There was no answer. Then she called Spiros.

"Hello?"

"Spiros, it's me."

"Are you all right?"

"Oh, yeah, just been running around all day. I'm upstate with the carpenter. Everything is set. Did you get a chance to look at the slides? I dropped them off Wednesday."

"Yes."

"Well?"

"Kate dear, it's difficult to see in the slides what the impact will be when all the images are spread out in front of me. But my first impression is that the piece seems to lack compositional restraint. There's no pictorial entrapment. No sense of archetonic space."

"Are you joking?"

Kate wanted a cigarette. When was the last time she had actually smoked one? She stuck her head out the kitchen door and made a rolling motion between her thumb and forefinger. Pearl smiled and threw her the pouch.

"What do you mean?"

That was the first question Spiros had ever asked her without affectation.

"I mean, Spiros, who wants to entrap photographs? Who cares about archetonic space when people are so sad?"

"Yes, yes, of course," he said, regaining his composure immediately. "Is something else bothering you?"

"Spiros, have you ever thought of me as a lesbian?"

"Absolutely not," he said without a pause. "You're an artist. You need a wide range of perverse experiences. No, absolutely not. Peter has been very busy with his work lately and you haven't been getting enough attention. But he'll take a vacation soon and I'm sure everything will go back to normal."

"Is that true?"

"Oh yes."

"Has he been extra busy lately?"

"Very busy. Now you calm down, Kate. Relax. Peter is a great artist. He's brilliant. And you are too. The world has not fully recognized the quality of work that the two of you produce because you are both speaking the truth and the world is stupid. All of the world's great artists were first ignored because they were too far ahead of their time. You're nervous about the installation, that's all."

She felt very small.

"Everything will be better, Kate, you'll see, I promise. Now be a good girl and get to sleep. Here's a kiss for you."

10
KATE

ΔΔΔΔΔΔΔΔΔΔΔΔΔΔΔΔΔΔΔΔΔΔΔΔΔΔΔΔΔΔΔΔΔΔΔΔΔΔΔΔΔΔΔΔΔΔΔΔΔΔΔΔΔΔΔΔΔΔΔΔΔΔΔΔΔΔΔΔΔΔΔΔΔΔ

Kate leaned back against the kitchen doorframe and inhaled her cigarette. It tasted great. When was the last time she had smoked? Probably the early seventies. Fifteen years? Was it possible not to have smoked a cigarette for fifteen years? Peter had smoked then too. He smoked Kents. They came in little gray packages that reminded her of the white shirts businessmen wore with suits. The cigarette packs were designed to peek out of the pockets of those kinds of shirts. What was the difference between love and habit? After a while one evolved into the other but how long ago had that happened? It was not a negative thing necessarily. You know how to act, he knows how to act. As long as neither of you changes everything is fine.

What had Peter looked like? She couldn't remember. He had been charming and skinny with a full head of hair. How long ago was that? What would happen if he found a kind of music she didn't like or gave her a book she didn't want to read? What if she went someplace on her own he'd never been before? What then? He never said what he wanted, he just looked unhappy and moped. Then she had to take care of him. There was nothing wrong with that, he would take care of her if she were in his shoes. He did the shopping sometimes when she told him what to get. He never cheated.

Then a graceful woman came slowly into the kitchen.

"Hi, I'm Becky. I just wanted to get some water."

"Hello," Kate said. "No problem, I'm finished in here."

She went back into the main room to sit with the two women for a while.

Becky and Pearl were quite lovely together, Kate had to admit, even though she disliked Pearl. Actually, she despised her. Pearl was in a ghetto. She was a man-hater. Still, Kate could aesthetically appreciate such luxurious hair and their glowing objective loveliness. Kate was universal and so she could enjoy and appreciate all forms of beauty and did so until they excused themselves to rush off to bed. From her chair Kate could hear them giggle and whisper and moan slightly. She missed Molly. She missed talking to her. She missed touching her. She heard the two women making love and thought about when she and Molly made love and could not accept that it was the same thing.

No matter how much I think about it or hear about it, no matter how much pain it causes me or how exciting it can be, it has not become acceptable for me. It is not regular.

The next morning she got up very early filled with energy and didn't know what to do with it. She went out and came back to sounds of Pearl and Becky making love again. She waited, static, until Pearl woke, dressed, ate and was ready to go to work.

They went out in back behind the work shed, where Pearl was storing the frames under large tarps. After hauling each one out and positioning it, Pearl began putting hinges on each piece and worked steadily while Kate spread out a sheet and sat on the grass. The woman Kate was watching at work had been an intoxicated lover the night before. But now Pearl was acting as though nothing had happened. Why wasn't she howling and dancing? That made Kate think how grown-up Pearl must be. Right then Kate established a definition of an adult as someone capable of making love and then going on, as though their writh-ing, wanting self belonged to a different life. At just that moment Pearl looked up from her thick legs and her utility belt. She looked right at Kate who could see and imagine Pearl's eyes at the same time. There was a clear flicker of laughter in the back-ground of her iris, vaguely reminiscent of her hands dripping in saliva, cum and blood. There was scent lingering on her fingers that revived her like a quick dip in a waterfall, as she casually passed her hand over her upper lip. How could Pearl be working so seriously? Kate was curious, imagining each woman's secret behind her most presentable self. But maybe it was just the light.

41

MOLLY

△△

There was no way that Molly could possibly sleep. The night was vibrating for her like a personalized set of Magic Fingers in a desolate hotel somewhere outside of Reno. She had been living in a box of closed possibilities and then it occurred to her quite suddenly that she did deserve love after all.

She put on her shoes, straightened out her place, made the bed, washed the glasses. She took out the garbage and stuffed it in the gray steel cans sitting on the street. But first Molly sorted out the bottles into separate bags and carefully laid them on the hood of a parked car so some homeless person could cash them in. That would make a nice after-midnight surprise for someone out of luck. Just when they were too tired to look through one more garbage bag there'd be enough bottles suddenly for a beer and two cigarettes. Most people throw their bottles out with the rest of the trash so bag pickers have to put their hands in rotting repulsive refuse for the five-cent deposit.

It was very late but not too hot. Many bodies were on the street and most of them were murmuring. The night rumbled like a human subway. People were sleeping everywhere and because it was warm, their corpses lay with outstretched bare limbs making small sounds, head protected by a newspaper or hand. She started walking among them in and out of yellow streetlights around the same old blocks. She talked to herself. She felt desire. She wanted to be close to a woman's body. Then she remembered something fantastic. She remembered that Sam was not Kate. She could call Sam anytime. She could just stop by her place. There was no guy keeping her from Sam's love. She walked straight and quickly talking herself all the way to Sam's door. There was no answer. There was no sound. So she went looking to find this woman in the purple night and take her home.

Molly checked out a few bars around the neighborhood and peeked into the bodegas. Then she walked Sam's area, systematically trying out streets she had never tried before at any time of day. It wasn't that she felt alone. It was that she was alone. It was that reality which reinforced her determination, being out there in the middle of the night and no one knew.

Only two things happened. There was a weird conversation with an old black man on a corner somewhere and then this flickering fluorescent light from Lillian's Coffee Shop on Second Street. It was a greasy light, like a dirty bathroom with no sink. Inside was a sign for homemade pie and a cowgirl who couldn't sleep, and so sat back instead bobbing drowsily over coffee and a slice of it. Her cigarette was burning in the metal ashtray and her eyes hung very low. Sam could have been downtown off any highway living out that 1950s beat reality in the middle of the last coffee shop in New York City that served their last piece of pie.

"I can't catch up," Sam said as Molly brought her back to her room. "There's nothing in modern life that grabs me."

They had both been drowning earlier that evening and doing it privately.

There is relief, Molly realized, smelling sweaty fruity scent at the base of Sam's neck. *Thank God.*

When Sam ate her she tasted every shape. She wasn't just

moving her tongue up and down. The more excited Molly became and the larger her clitoris swelled, the lighter was Sam's tongue, pulling back, always, to the surface, which gave Molly a chance for real feeling, not just pressure and quickness. Women's cunts are so different from each other, Molly knew each had to be felt thoroughly to find out about the person surrounding it. Sam knew about the little things, like pulling up Molly's stomach every now and then so her clit would stretch flat and then letting it slide back again. Sam knew how to make love so that by the end of it there were sore cunts and assholes and nipples and lips dripping. There was no deep need still lingering, only tenderness and then a crazy serenity.

"Talked to Daisy about your girlfriend," Sam said, looking right then like a very beautiful quiet woman with soft breasts. "She said you've been suffering."

"I don't want to go into that too much right now," Molly said. "Because I'm happy to be with you. You feel so good to me."

Sam didn't talk a lot. She wasn't that way. The feelings came through sometimes without too many words and they were often unknown.

"It's all right to be upset," Sam said.

"I am upset." Molly started to shake. She felt so comfortable. "I'm very upset." She was trembling and then cold. Her muscles were twitching. She didn't know how to make them stop until Sam opened up her body.

"Take my heat," she said.

Her voice gave Molly permission to relax into her and let Sam's warmth penetrate her deeply.

It feels good to be safe, she thought. *I feel so happy to be safe. When I'm intimate with another person I always learn something. If it's with someone I can grow to love, the things I learn are so beautiful they lift me. Being close smells cool and sweet. It feels great, feels so warm.*

Molly took hold of the scruff of Sam's neck.

This is just what I need, she thought. And then she said so out loud.

42
MOLLY

"I don't have to go to work until eleven," Sam said. "Let's do something great. Let's get stoned and go to Central Park."

"I can't," Molly said, rolling over Sam's flesh to get to her clothes. "It's credit card day."

"What's that?"

"It's Justice. Justice strikes today. How come you never come to meetings? Doesn't Trudy tell you what's going on?"

"What's going on?"

"Thousands of people are dropping dead and no one cares. People won't do anything until it affects them. That's what's going on, Sam."

"It's ugly," Sam said.

"Yeah," Molly said. "But it's real."

Molly looked at Sam's green eyes, the way they twinkled. She looked at iron muscles and little pieces of flesh.

"We're so lucky, Sam. We're so lucky we don't have to watch each other die."

Sam got dressed then, slowly. She put on her bolo tie and followed Molly out onto the street, locking all the locks behind them.

"We've been planning this for a long time," Molly said. "I don't know if I can honestly say 'we' because I didn't do the most. I just do a little bit every now and then. But that makes me part of it."

"You think a little bit now and then is okay?" Sam asked.

"Yeah," Molly said. "But only because there are a lot of people in Justice, so a lot of little bits is a lot. If there were only a few, then even doing it all the time wouldn't be enough."

They got down quickly to the big twenty-four-register Pathmark sitting in a parking lot by the waterfront on Cherry Street near the projects. There were a lot of homeless people hanging out in front. They were the kind of people who were usually hanging out but not in that exact spot. And it wasn't in their exact way either. They weren't passing time and they weren't scrounging. They were, instead, expecting. They weren't loitering. They appeared to be gathering.

Molly ran up to Fabian, deep in negotiation at the front of the crowd.

"How did this happen?"

"Molly, good, Bob needs you to help by the poultry counter."

Fabian was fully decked out in leather cutouts, chaps, boots with spurs and a series of bandannas in a variety of colors.

"How did all these people get here?"

"Mario and Roger went out last night leafleting the welfare hotels and the Third Street men's shelter. People were lining up hours before we got here, just wanting to see what would happen. It's scary when you put out the call and the people actually show up. If we don't deliver, this crowd is going to be real pissed off."

"So . . . ?"

"So, go help out Bob. He's got chicken cutlets coming out of his ears."

Sam went around to check out the back and Molly made her way through the men. It was mostly men. Young men. There were some women and they had kids with them but most of the men came alone. Some smelled so badly she retched. She almost threw up from the smell. Someone asked her for money, she said no. Some people were all right, but some people stank of urine.

Bob had his hands full with papers and a disoriented Pathmark staff. He was easy to spot, being so tall and silver in a Stetson and a red and white checked shirt with silver-rimmed pearl snaps.

"Molly, this is Mario. This is Don. They are our Chinese- and Spanish-language interpreters. We're expecting a whole Chinatown contingent any minute and we have extra take-home wagons available for families who have to walk long distances."

They all shook hands.

"I'm afraid we're in a slight state of chaos here. So, Molly, figure out a way to get people to line up so they can get in touch with the appropriate translator."

The three of them went back into the crowd and Molly tried yelling, "Line up, line up," but that didn't work.

"That's not going to work," Mario said.

Right then the Chinese contingent arrived, mostly older women with stacks of empty shopping bags.

Don yelled something out in Chinese.

"What did you say?" Molly asked.

"I said, 'Line up, line up.' "

"Didn't work," Mario said.

Finally Bob stood up on the back of a delivery truck and yelled through a bullhorn.

"If you want free food be quiet now!"

That worked.

"Okay," Bob said. "The following food is available for free: meat, fish, chicken, all protein, cheese, eggs, dairy, beans, flour, rice, fresh fruit, vegetables, good bread, real juice, nuts, peanut butter, spice, oils and other whole foods. Also vitamins. And remember this supermarket sweepstakes is brought to you by none other than the friendly faggots and dykes of Justice."

Then Mario and Don did quick translations.

The crowd became unexpectedly attentive and well behaved, although there was a definite undercurrent of "wait and see" about all of it. Molly remembered Sam and then found out she was right there beside her.

"The closest thing I've ever seen to this before," Sam said, "was waiting on line for five hours in the cold to get ten pounds of that goddamn cheese the government was giving away. Remember? It wasn't even good cheese. It was that orange waxy kind."

"When you get to the checkout counter," Bob continued, "and the hardworking woman at the machine asks you how you intend to pay, just tell her 'Charge it.' Repeat after me: '*Charge it!*'"

And everybody did.

"There we go, a little more group spirit can never hurt. Then, I'll put your bill on these American Express cards. The actual owners of these cards are unable to be with us today because they are in the hospital. But they send their love and authorization to all of you. Okay, easy does it. Now, let's go."

Fortunately Mario, Molly, Don, Sam, Bob and Fabian all had the same thought at the same moment, which was to get the hell out of the way, because the men and women came bursting through the front doors with such fury that the shatterproof plate-glass windows shuddered in their frames.

The Justice boys and girls took turn running like crazy up and down the checkout lines shuffling plastic back and forth.

"Don't leave home without it," Fabian said, every time their paths crossed.

People went straight for the meat, of course. But once they had it in their baskets they allowed themselves some long-ago-forgotten pleasures like peaches. Or ice cream. There is food that fills you up and then there is food that tastes so good in the mouth it makes a person feel human again. It brings back memories. It reminds a guy of other things.

After half an hour, Bob came panting over to where the girls were handing out credit slips.

"We're almost all out of everything of nutritional value," he gasped. "All that's left is junk."

"There are still people coming in the door," Sam called over her shoulder.

"Well, we can't be unduly moralistic," Don said. "Let people take whatever they want, even if it is Fritos and Diet Coke. I mean, when you need to eat, you need to eat."

So Don and Mario and Bob got back on the megaphone and that set off another rush, only this time for frozen pizza, Spam, hot dogs and Cool Whip.

"Now what?" Molly asked when Fabian ran up with a worried expression.

"People who only got fresh meat and good vegetables are complaining," he said. "Because they really wanted Twinkies."

After an emergency consultation the crew decided they had no right to tell people what to eat. They could only make suggestions and immediate happiness was not a negligible goal, so they let the first-timers go through again for their sugar fix. Bob couldn't let go completely though, so he sat by the freezer section yelling out "Häagen-Dazs, Häagen-Dazs!" hoping to have some influence.

"This is an issue we have to seriously consider in the future," Mario said. "This cannot be denied."

When the last bottle of Thousand Island dressing was taken and the last can of pork and beans and the last jar of Fluff was packed into a carrier bag, Bob handed over one of the well-worn credit cards to a guy who had only gotten a six-pack of Good 'N Plenty.

"Do something truly inspired with this card," Bob said, totally exhausted. "Do something fabulous."

When the last person left and the Pathmark staff had crashed on each of the checkout-line conveyor belts, the men and women of Justice stood, together, silently holding on to one another and looking over the empty white cavern, watching the fluorescent lights ricochet off the empty shelves.

"It kind of looks like a monstrous, empty refrigerator," Fabian said.

"We're doing something real important," Don said. "We're making a difference today and it's not as hard as I thought it would be."

"Yeah, well," Mario said. "It seems like a big deal right now but tomorrow it will be over. I've been in politics a long time and little actions like this only work if they inspire people on to bigger ones."

On the way to the subway Don and Molly started to chat it up a bit because this was Don's first political experience and he was excited no matter what Mario said. Besides, they had seen each other at lots of meetings but had never gotten a chance to talk before.

"So, do you have a boyfriend?" Molly asked.

"My boyfriend died four years ago," Don said. "I've had a hard time getting another one because no one wants to get emotionally involved with someone who might die. But I don't want to take that stupid test, so every time I'm on a date I have to decide whether to tell them or not."

They put their tokens into the slots and gave coins to a musician, even though they couldn't hear a thing over the subway roar. Sam was there too but she didn't say much.

"Look at all the people on this train," Don said. "Think any of them will hear about what we've done?"

"Some. A few. A couple probably."

"Which ones?"

"The ones who read page ten of the *Daily News*."

He was drinking juice out of a carton and offered her some. She took it.

"So, do you think I should get the test? What do you think, Molly?"

"How will you feel if you're positive?"

"Depressed."

"How will you feel if you don't know?"

"I feel fine, really."

"It's up to you. I mean, if you find someone who really cares about you, it probably won't matter if you take it or not."

"I think I'll wait. I don't feel like being hysterical for the next three years."

"Good idea."

When Don got off the train Molly sat back quietly with her hand in Sam's lap.

"Why did you drink out of his carton when he might have AIDS?"

"It's a rite of passage. People who may be HIV positive inevitably offer you a drink out of their glass. It's a test of loyalty to see if you're prejudiced or not, to see if you are informed enough to know that you can't get it that way."

"That roommate I told you about?" Sam said. "The one who died?"

"Yeah."

"He shit all over himself and I had to clean it up. He was too sick to move so he had to lie in it until I got home."

Molly put her arm around Sam and buried her face in her neck.

"Sam, are you afraid?"

"I don't know," she said. "I don't know what I feel."

43

PETER

ΔΔΔΔΔΔΔΔΔΔΔΔΔΔΔΔΔΔΔΔΔΔΔΔΔΔΔΔΔΔΔΔΔΔΔΔΔΔΔΔΔΔΔΔΔΔΔΔΔΔΔΔΔΔΔΔΔΔΔΔΔΔΔΔΔΔΔΔΔΔΔΔΔΔΔΔ

That night Shelley sat next to Peter in an audience. She looked beautiful. She was charming with the people they met and she held her hand discreetly on his thigh throughout the entire third act. Afterward he took her backstage and showed her what a gel frame looks like, and a color wheel. He took her up into the booth and showed her how a dimmer board works. He explained how to cross-fade, how to sneak one in. He briefly mentioned plugging and showed a trick way to wrap a cable. She wasn't afraid to go up on the catwalk. In fact, she loved it.

"Maybe I can get you a job on a new production. That would be more fun than working at a Xerox store, don't you think? You can be an electrician."

"Pete, how could I do that? I don't know anything about electricity."

"It's easy. I'll teach you. I'll teach you in a week."

I could make her life so much more exciting, he thought. *I*

could teach her so many things. Maybe she'll get really good and we can work together until she becomes a designer on her own.

It felt great having Shelly in his bed. She absolutely belonged there. Her hair looked beautiful so long and full against the sheets.

"Look at those books on your night table," she said. "Derrida, yuch. I tried to read that for semiotics, sophomore year."

"You took semiotics?"

"I dropped it. Then I took women's studies instead. Bataille? Yuch. I tried to read that, the one about the eye. All he kept talking about was cramming, ramming and stuffing his cock inside some woman. Is this what you read before you go to bed? Well, it's a good way to fall asleep."

"Somebody's got to keep the university presses in business," he chuckled. "And somebody's got to keep intellectuals off the streets. Besides, it gives me deconstructed dreams." He laughed aloud.

"Are you teasing me?"

Her breasts were mostly nipple, long thin pink ones.

"It's not that difficult, really. Do you want me to explain it to you?"

He reached for his glasses.

"No. I mean, not now. Can you turn on the radio please?"

She sang along with a couple of songs, beating the drum machine parts out on his chest with her long red fingernails.

"Pete, do you like Sinhead?"

"Skinhead?"

"No, no. Oh, I love this song. Turn it up."

He tried to listen but he couldn't make out the words. When the song was over he switched to a tape and put in a cassette of Sonny Rollins.

"Does Kate read these books too?"

"Yes. She reads everything I read. That's why we always have something to talk about." He twisted her brown curls between his fingers. "We had to be like Jean-Paul and Simone or Frida and Diego."

"Who are Frida and Diego?"

"A famous art couple. The temptation of being geniuses to-gether becomes an excuse to stay together years after the relationship is over."

He looked into Shelley's deep brown eyes. How long had it been since he'd looked into brown eyes that way? He had her full attention.

"I love her," he said. "Because of all the time spent together, but I'm very angry. I'm not going to think about that right now though because I'd rather enjoy being with you."

"Peter," Shelley said. "It's okay to get upset, you know. It's just as normal to have feelings as it is to have ideas."

"I'm so upset," he said. "I'm really very upset." Then he folded into her and shook. Then he turned his back. Shelley wrapped around him. When he felt her heat on his back he relaxed. He knew she wanted to take care of him.

This is a way of being close that is different from the way that Kate and I are close, he thought. This is not rooted in nostalgia or habit or familiarity or fear of being alone, or logistics, or shared business or obligation. It's just comfort. When you are intimate with another person you find another way of loving and it becomes part of you.

"You're wonderful, Shelley. You're being so great about this."

"Well the way I see it," she said, "is that this is a kind of unusual situation that I have gotten myself into and I'm going to have a lot of different unusual experiences in my life, because, I mean, we're not going to get married or anything and I don't plan on being normal or boring. Do you understand what I mean? I'm not saying it right."

"I understand."

"Hey, Peter?"

"Yeah."

"There's a strange guy standing at the foot of the bed."

Peter jumped out, not knowing quite why. His half-erect penis was flopping, which confused him even more and he went straight into the bathroom without looking either woman in the eye. They saw each other though, and not with much malice.

"I'm very tired," Kate said. "I hope you will excuse me."

With that she took off her suit jacket and unsnapped her suspenders. She unbuttoned her shirt and trousers and dropped them on the floor. Then, kicking off her big black shoes, she walked over to the bed in her T-shirt and cotton boxer shorts and climbed in.

"Let's go," Peter said, hustling Shelley out of bed.

"What do you want?" Shelley asked Kate as one woman got out and the other slid in.

"When I wake up," Kate said, pulling up the rumpled covers, "I want you both to be gone."

44

PETER

△△△

Justice had gotten too large for the bathhouse, so they crashed the Saint, a three-story nightclub, former gay bar extraordinaire that used to be the Filmore East that used to be a Loew's and was about to become a Cineplex triplex complex where anyone could see three bad movies for the price of four. Three generations of underground people had had extreme experiences in that building.

When Justice stormed in, they disrupted a power networking party organized by the Business Association of Single Traders and Retail Distributors of Saccharine. The sight of over one thousand passionate pederasts and sodomites in black T-shirts and the word *Justice* spray-painted over pink triangles encouraged most of the BASTARDS to leave by the fire exits. The management didn't care who was in the place as long as they bought drinks. Justice poured into the third-story dance floor, filled the gray-carpeted balconies which were the site of a quarter of a million precrisis blow jobs, until they were filled. The overflow crowd watched the meeting on video screens from the tastefully lit silver and gray bar area.

Molly didn't see Kate anywhere. She didn't want to see her but she did want to. She knew for sure, though, that Kate wasn't there because Molly could always see Kate coming, no matter how large the crowd and certainly miles before Kate could see her. It was her hair that burned like a fiery halo, a glowing ember. She walked in burning amidst a sea of light brown blah.

Daisy called the meeting to order.

"If there is anyone here from the Federal Bureau of Investigation or the New York City Police Department, drop dead." The audience howled. They were ready to cheer at anything. Molly knew that she and Kate had to talk, or better yet, Kate had to listen. Standing up to her was so difficult. Kate had a side that was well-bred and properly ladylike, which she used when she was too tired to interact. She'd smile prettily then, show her teeth for a moment and then cover them demurely with her lips, which she kept soft. She'd look you in the eye during all of this, so as not to appear evasive, and she'd speak clearly, offering nothing. If someone pressed her, the wall came down. There were times when being with Kate was like being on the wrong side of a Plexiglas sheet. There were times when you could dance with her and she would give you nothing. She wouldn't move with you or against you. She moved apart from you. But it all seemed to be within her grasp, a matter of choice. She could hide behind her beauty and then, suddenly, fight you fiercely, cruelly, brutally with a complete determination to win.

"Now with the credit car report, Cardinal Spellman."

The little guy struggled up onto the platform in his scarlet cape and red velvet cap.

"That's Miss Spellman to you," he said, raising his hand in a sign of Christian peace and then letting it flap at the wrist. "Hail Mary and Helen too." He threw some holy seltzer on the crowd and read his report.

"Let's see, well, there was this frantic food buyout at Pathmark, then a number of fur coats were purchased at Bergdorf's and distributed to residents of the women's shelter. Plumbing, electrical and construction supplies for the Lower East Side squatters were charged at Broadway Lumber until the raised letters on the Visa card got rubbed off from too many charge slips. James was stationed at Liberty Travel where many one-way tickets were issued for people wanting to go home or even better places. Most popular destinations were Jamaica, Puerto Rico and Miami Beach. I would also like to say personally, as someone with ARC, that charging the hell out of New York City with no intention to pay is a fabulous way to work out your anger. Now where are my altar boys?''

A number of scantily clad teenagers appeared in loincloths, hoisted her excellency up on a huge Plexiglas cross and hauled her away in a sea of kisses.

"Oh Father," cooed Miss Spellman. "Oh Son. Oh Holy Holy Ghost."

When the applause died down, Daisy came back to take the mike.

"There are times when you have to dream," Daisy said. "And then speak those dreams. Here are mine."

Molly remembered where she was. She was with her people. She couldn't let Kate take her out of herself ever again.

"I dream," Daisy continued, "that by tomorrow at three in the afternoon, American Express, Visa and Mastercard's stocks will have tumbled so low, they will fall off the charts. Then the entire board of directors of each company will be forced to resign with a large majority taking the easy way out via cyanide pills. The Dow Jones will close early so all the brokers can rush home and smoke crack while the banks repossess their BMWs and their health club memberships and foreclose on their condominiums which used to be your rent-controlled apartments. By Wednesday, noon, the military-industrial complex will be reduced to rubble. There will be homes for the homeless, food for the hungry, care for the ill, permission for the imagination and no weapons. Then I'll go home, light a joint, open a beer and make love for the rest of my life. How does that sound to you?''

There was an explosion then of shared joy. There were many expectations in that room that night in the occupied, air-conditioned disco.

"Remember that feeling," Daisy said. "Hold on to that dream while James shares a few words."

James came to the front of the room. He was very tired. His clothes were dirty. He looked unkempt. His spirit was failing him, everyone could see that. They were very, very quiet then. You could hear a thousand people holding their collective breath.

"Please listen to me critically," he said. He didn't start by saying "brothers and sisters," which was what he usually said. He started by saying "Please." He seemed frightened. Molly had never seen this emotion in his face before. Like someone looking out over a sea of faces knowing that each one of them had an expectation he had to live up to. There was more trust than one person could bear.

"There is a euphoria in taking control of your own life. There is something crippling that occurs when the response to that act distorts it. As long as the people fighting for change are smaller than the institutions that control information, their activities will be misrepresented, their impact minimized and their humanity questioned. The only way to overcome the machinery is to become bigger than it is. So that, one day, more people will be participating in the event than watching it on television. That is called a revolution. In the meantime we are placated with a condition of free speech in a nation of no ideas."

The room held an arched silence. Even people with drinks in their hands never lifted the glasses to their mouths.

"Let me read to you now from the front page of tomorrow's newspaper, smuggled to us by a lesbian working at the printing plant. The headline says 'AIDS Victims Riot in City.' "

Molly wanted to be held. She wanted arms around her and they weren't Kate's because Molly wanted to be safe right then. That's what she needed most in the world.

" 'Marauding bands of AIDS victims roamed the city today looting. Real-estate magnate Ronald Horne, announcing his decision to run for mayor, told the press that he advocated barge internment camps for all those infected with the deadly AIDS virus. Horne said he would personally finance and administer this quarantine program to show his love for the people of New York. He added that any apartments in Horne-owned buildings that might be left vacant due to internment would immediately be converted to luxury co-ops for intact nuclear families, which statistics show are the least likely to spread AIDS. He will present more details at the Thursday afternoon inauguration of the Taj McHorne, a new office and condominium complex on the site of the old public library.' "

James looked out carefully at the crowd before he spoke again. He wanted to really see them, to look in their faces.

"I know where I'm going to be Thursday afternoon. Do you?"

"Yes," they said.

They didn't all say it the first time but when he asked again, they did.

"Yes," they said.

"In that case," he answered, "let's dance."

45

MOLLY

ΔΔΔΔΔΔΔΔΔΔΔΔΔΔΔΔΔΔΔΔΔΔΔΔΔΔΔΔΔΔΔΔΔΔΔΔΔΔΔΔΔΔΔΔΔΔΔΔΔΔΔΔΔΔΔΔΔΔΔΔΔΔΔΔΔΔΔΔΔΔ

Scott Yarrow 1958–1988 died of pneumonia resulting from pneumocystis, an AIDS-related opportunistic infection. Only a few of
his friends found out early enough to be able to make it to the
hospital before he died. Molly was one of them. Fabian was the
other, because he brought Scott to Bellevue emergency room.
When the nurse took Scott in on a stretcher behind the swinging
doors, Fabian madly made telephone calls until he could find
someone to come sit with him in that hellhole.

During the four hours that Molly and Fabian sat, many events
occurred. There were a number of street people sleeping, crying,
with gangrene, with large infections, with snot covering their
faces, with blood everywhere, unable to speak, unable to move,
all unattended and with no place to go. There were a few gunshots
brought in by the police. A man had been beaten up. His friend
had one arm around him and another arm holding the stack of
records that they had been on their way to spin. Mothers worried

they had waited too long. A man urinated in his pants. Many were drinking. Some were talking very loudly about very little. The police brought in a few cases from Riker's Island—pale men in bright orange jumpsuits with manacles, leg and ankle chains. There were many, many drug overdoses. A man sat behind Molly masturbating for the entire four hours. He never got off. There were terrible smells.

One of the prisoners was unusually large. He had a scar clear across his throat. From where he was sitting he could stare directly at Molly. He kept motioning to her, waving. At first she smiled back, feeling sorry for him, then she realized that he was going to be waving at her all afternoon and she had other things to think about.

She and Fabian knew Scott was dying but they didn't talk about it much.

"My lover died of pneumocystis," Fabian said. "His name was Jay. He went like that." Fabian snapped his fingers and looked down at the filthy floor. "At the end he wouldn't eat. I got so frustrated with him I would say 'Goddammit Jay, eat.' But he wouldn't."

During the day a few other people came in with AIDS. You could tell it was AIDS because they were too thin and weak for their age or else their faces were covered with those lesions. Finally James came. It took him a while to convince the staff that he was immediate family, but a friendly nurse let him in.

"I got tested a few months ago, you know," Fabian said.

"No, I didn't know."

"I waited a while because those tests are so crazy. You never know what they're going to do with the results and you never know if the results are even right."

"So, what happened?"

"I tested positive."

"Now what?" Molly slipped her arm around his shoulder and leaned her head there.

"Well, I read in *The New England Journal of Medicine* that there are a couple of experimental protocols for drugs you can start taking when you're only at the positive stage. But there aren't many available spots in the program. So, I'm trying to switch to a more influential doctor who can get me into one of them. But I might have to move to another city and being lonely could get me sick faster, don't you think?"

Molly didn't say anything. So the two of them just sat there with their heads together for a while.

Then Fabian went off to get a Coke and one of the homeless guys came up to Molly with a note from the prisoner with the healed slit throat. It was written in pencil with that kind of handwriting people have when they don't really know how to write. It said

Hi There!
    My name is Frank Castillo No #241-86-1885. I have about four to five months to do in here. If you write me I will write you. I have been in jail for twenty-eight months and haven't had no woman since. You are very pretty. I would also like to call you. I will pay for the call. Please think about it. I am really not a bad person.

Molly stared at this note for a long time, except for every once in a while when she forgot and raised her eyes accidentally. Whenever that happened, Frank would be there with his hand-cuffed hands put together in prayer and him saying "Please, please, please" silently with his fat lips.

I can't take care of everybody, Molly said to herself. *I just can't. I can't do it. This is one of those times that I have to say no.*

So she looked up at Frank and mouthed "No" because even when the answer is no, people deserve a response. But he just sent her another note. It said

I'm sorry if I embarrassed you. I just want to talk to you. If you give me your phone number I can call you and we might become good friends. The officer said it would be all right for you to talk to me.
                        Frank

She looked up again accidentally and he was right there mouthing "Please, please, please" again. So finally Molly took out another piece of paper and wrote the following note.

Dear Frank,
You seem to be a very open person. I just can't pursue this relationship with you because I am a lesbian and I have learned from past experiences that whenever I make friends with a straight man they always want more. I hope you meet the woman who is right for you. I hope I do too.

She didn't sign it. She just sent it back to him by messenger and then changed her seat so she didn't have to watch him read it with his handcuffs on.

Then Fabian came back with his Coke and drank it and they were still waiting. Then James came out and Scott was dead. The three of them held one another very close and then looked at each other and there was already something missing. From then on, Scott would not be there.

"He waited for me," James said as they walked down along the East River. There was some wealthy private school on the water, so wherever they walked there were packs of bilingual boys and girls in dark blue jackets and skirts. There was an expensive restaurant, some luxury housing and a heliport for businessmen from powerful companies. Fabian held James's hand as he talked. The sun reflected off the water with great freshness and clarity. There was light everywhere. The promenade overflowed with human movement and warm pleasure.

"He should have been gone by the time I got there but he was still hanging on. I saw death when I looked at him. His eyes were yellow. There was nothing left inside. I took his hand and brought my face right up to his, like we were kissing. Really close, like when we sleep and my nose is buried in his cheek. I breathed on him. My eyes were on his eyes. I know he felt me. I took his hand and squeezed it. I said, 'Scott, can you see me? Can you see me?' until I knew he saw and then I said, 'I love you. I love you, Scott. I love you.' And I watched him die, knowing he was a loved person in this world. That was the last thing he knew."

They left James at his front door and after Molly left a long composed letter in Kate's mailbox, she and Fabian walked on a little way together over to the West Side and down Christopher Street. They were pretty quiet except when Fabian stopped to buy an ice cream cone. It was another gay summer and they were in it. There were all those sexy guys prancing around. Some of them were sweet young things wearing practically nothing. Some of them were big hunks wearing practically nothing. The usual fag teenagers were hanging out by the water playing radios and lots of guys in bicycle pants were cruising around, being cute. A few straight women were walking around with their gay friends talking things over and one voyeuristic straight couple clung to each other desperately.

"This is where I first saw Scott," Molly said. "It was about a year ago. He and James were handing out flyers for Justice. Scott had long hair then and a big Pepsodent smile. I remember I was mad at Kate for not being around. A year has passed. Not much has changed."

"This is where I first met Scott too," Fabian said. "About six years ago at the Ramrod. He blew me on the pier."

"It's been a long year," Molly said. "A huge one. But nothing much has changed."

16
KATE

△△

Dear Kate,
Scott died this morning. Life is very short. I can't
waste mine waiting for you to love me enough. There's
something missing in you. I don't think you know how
to love. You just know how to hold on to people. It's
not the same thing.

She heard the door to James's apartment start to open and
she knew she didn't want to see him. Still holding the letter Kate
stepped back quietly under the staircase and waited until he was
out the front door. He was walking with a black woman Kate
had never seen before and she only heard snippets of their conversation. She heard two things: "Why me?" and "I don't want
to die."
She was sweating. She walked outside and noticed everything. The buses had been painted a new color. There was a new

△△△

song on the radio. All the kids were singing it. She passed two parks filled with street people drinking or sleeping or smoking Coke or cigarettes or crying or talking to themselves and to others or dying. She sat with them for a while, once in each park, and smelled their urine and sweat. Every garbage can on Second Avenue had been picked through. She saw the headline on a newsstand: AIDS VICTIMS RIOT.

Three elderly women asked her for money. She gave them everything she had. Then she went to the bank machine and got out more. Four times young men tried to sell her drugs. In each case she bought what they offered without inspection and dropped three bags of marijuana and one crack vial on the sidewalk. There was trash everywhere. The streets were broken and filled with holes. There was a hooker on Twelfth Street who was clutching her vagina and crying. Kate unlocked the front door to her studio. Her skin was burning. It was bubbling up and blistering. It was dripping brown fat. Her arms were dislocated and skin became plaster, then a greasy foreign substance. Her clitoris was as big as her hand. No, bigger. It filled the universe between her ankles and her groin. It had no temperature and moved of its own accord. Then she felt nothing.

Kate walked into her studio and Peter was there. He wore a clean cotton button-down shirt, freshly ironed.

"What are you doing, Katie? I don't understand you. You don't care about anything unless it's gay. You don't think about anything unless it's gay. I'm really surprised that you would become so narrow."

She took a step toward him.

"I understand you feel a need to be politically active but I think that is something we can do together. Homosexuals don't have a monopoly on morality, you know. We have always agreed that our artwork is our political work. We have always agreed that challenging form is more revolutionary than any political organization ever can be. But if you feel a need to be part of a group, we can do that together. I mean, I care more about Nicaragua than I do about a group of rich white gay men. Wouldn't you like to work together on something less exclusive?"

She pressed her face into his chest. His shoulders were like guard rails. She was surrounded by him. She had no air.

"That girl means nothing to me," he said. "Nothing. You give up yours and I'll give up mine. Then we can be exactly like we were before."

She placed her fingers flat against his chest. It was a wall. It moved. There was hair underneath his shirt. She wanted to dig her fingernails in and tear him apart.

He spoke again. What did he say this time?

47
KATE

△△

The *New York Times* obituary said that Scott was "survived" by two daughters, a wife, mother, father and sister in Kansas City. Then Kate found a privately placed notice at the bottom of the obituary page.

Scott Yarrow died in the arms of his lover, James Carroll, with whom he shared a vision of freedom for lesbians and gay men.

When she went to the site of the funeral, Kate discovered that it was the same church where she had watched Molly and Pearl months before. Now she too was a mourner. There were so many people it was impossible to even consider getting into the church. Once inside, what would they do there anyway? "Ashes to ashes, dust to dust" had no place here. There was only fire. Kate looked closely at the crowd. There were some people she knew from Justice meetings. Fabian and Bob were there. So were Cardinal Spellman and Trudy and Daisy. But most of the faces were unknown to her. These people did not greet one another. There were no words. They did not touch. There were no embraces, only anger and a shared determination that passed between them.

Six men emerged carrying Scott's coffin. It seemed to be as light as air. They began passing the box over the heads of the crowd as each one reached out to touch the wood like it was the Torah. His encased body passed through the hands of his people on its way to burial. It was placed in the hearse without eulogy or speeches.

As the car inched away the crowd parted and then, like one person, began walking silently to Fifth Avenue, turning up it toward the library. They walked in the street against traffic. Kate could feel the exhaust of idling cars against her calves. Her lungs were filled with it. She climbed over cars, disregarded them. When there are that many people the traffic can't move. When that many people walk together the traffic has to stop. At first the drivers cursed, but soon rolled up their windows and sat still in disgust listening to their radios.

The men and women arrived at the library and stopped there in front of the old granite lions. Everyone looked up at the huge stained-glass windows that once let in light on halls of free books and old wooden reading tables. They stood very, very quietly.

Horne had already started speaking from a raised platform, where he sat on a pile of cushions dressed as a raja in accord with the India-themed decor of the renovated library. Now it would be a health club for businessmen working in midtown. The main reading room had become a large sauna and the rare book room, handball courts. Horne was speaking into the microphone, it didn't matter what he was saying. The edges of the stage were guarded by some young white thugs in brownface with guns in their pantaloons and walkie-talkies under their turbans. But five guns couldn't kill a thousand people. Kate saw plastic boa constrictors and college students hired to be dancing girls. Everyone on the stage was just working a job.

Horne stopped for a moment to look out at the solid mass before him. He had an expression on his face that Kate recognized from television. It was a practiced glibness. He was searching for just the right throwaway comment to invalidate all the people in front of him and at the same time make great copy for the front page of the next day's *New York Post*. But nothing very clever seemed to come to mind. He started sweating a bit, then, and took a drink of water.

Kate saw James climbing up on Bob's shoulders. The contrast of black skin and silver hair made a momentary impression on her. James turned toward the audience and spoke evenly, not trying to outshout anyone. The crowd was pretty antsy anyway and looking for some direction, so they kept still and listened carefully.

"If you instigate chaos," he said, "make sure that it is to your advantage or that you have no other choice."

Then they roared. The black T-shirts with pink triangles swarmed over the equipment, smashing it. They trampled the press section, throwing the cameras into the street and stomping on them. There would be no observers this time. Everyone would participate or run. Kate climbed up on top of an overturned Cable News Network van and was surprised by the sight of her own artwork, spread out behind Horne's platform. The private body-guards were jumping off the stage, flying against the background of her collage, leaving Horne alone, retreating until he was wrapped by her images. Reinforcements started arriving from the police department and were beginning to surround the crowd. The cops were still on the outside but there was very little time left for someone to act in a large way. People were already at the edges of the platform, leaving Horne and her pictures trapped. Then he pulled out a gun. The men who had begun climbing up on the stage pulled back, quickly, and hovered on the wood, swinging their legs over the sides. Kate pushed harder than she had ever pushed and clawed her way to the front of the stage, catching and tearing her flesh on the splintered police sawhorses that lay mangled everywhere. Then she climbed under it, crawling on the dirt and garbage over wires, rags, cans of paint and turpentine. She watched her own hands turn black and her arms cake with dirt and blood surrounded by the moving spikes of pants legs bobbing around her. Dragging the cans and power lines to the base of the collage's wooden frames, she looked back at the chaos behind her. Each gesture was too large and so unusual that the action passed before her like a high-speed silent film. Only there was no silence.

∆∆

18

▵▵▵

ROLAND

Good evening, ladies and gentlemen, welcome to Channel Z News. I'm Roland Johnson.

SUSIE

And I'm Susie Fong.

AL

Al Harber with sports.

CASPER

And Doctor Casper Griffin with the weather.

ROLAND

All this and more when Channel Z continues after this message.

[Commercial]

ROLAND

Good evening. In the news tonight, Ronald Horne murdered in Forty-second Street melee. Congress approves new Contra aid plan. Mayor goes to bat for the peanut butter bagel and Masters and Johnson warn heterosexuals: new threat from AIDS. But first, Susie?

SUSIE

Thank you, Roland. Real-estate mogul Ronald Horne met a fiery death today when a freak accident occurred during a riot by AIDS victims. An art installation designed for the inauguration of a new health club caught fire and enveloped the billionaire developer in a flaming collage. Police are still investigating the incident. We switch live to Sonny Harris on location in Bryant Park. Sonny?

SONNY

Thank you, Susie. Little remains of today's riot except for the scattered scraps of television equipment smashed by the angry mob. We are here with Chief of Command Ed Ramsey of Manhattan South. Chief, can you tell us what happened?

ED RAMSEY

At approximately two twelve this afternoon, a piece of art that had been placed in the park caught on fire. The artist has informed us that he was using polyurethane, a known flammable substance.

SONNY

Thank you, Chief Ramsey. Back to you, Roland.

ROLAND

Thanks, Sonny. Congress voted today to approve a multimillion-dollar aid package to rebel forces in Nicaragua. Frank Miller has details from Washington. Frank?

19

MOLLY

△△△

As soon as Molly caught sight of Kate's hair, she'd climbed up on a lamppost and kept her eyes pinned to that woman throughout the entire event. She'd seen Kate go under the stage and then come out again on the other side and watched her slip under the framing just as the first flames began to appear. Then Kate had come around to behind the police lines and watched the fire from across the street.

For a few weeks after the event Molly had vague thoughts of seeing Kate again but had never acted on it and eventually any desire toward her faded, naturally. She wasn't even provoked by curiosity as Kate developed a high profile as a result of Horne's death and could be read about in an essay by Gary Indiana in the *Village Voice* and one by Barbara Kruger in *ArtForum*. In fact, Kate began working extensively in burning installations and quickly got commissions from a number of Northern European countries to come start fires there. She had been in Amsterdam for six months working on a blazing sculpture in honor of the people of Cambodia when Peter came up to Molly in a coffee shop on Ninth Street.

It had been a long winter for Molly. She spent a lot of it alone and was relatively quiet. Both Fabian and Daisy were dead by Thanksgiving. Fabian had wanted a drug called M-Reg One. But the FDA killed it in phase-three trials. Daisy ended up on AZT, which she couldn't really tolerate and her legs went so numb that she could barely walk. They both died angry.

"Hi, Molly, how are you?" Peter said, being friendly. Then he sat down next to her at the counter and started talking about the new play he was working on. He also mentioned that he wasn't getting the recognition he deserved and wasn't getting paid what he was worth.

Molly tried to ignore him. Then a pretty woman came into the coffee shop and kissed Peter on the mouth.

"Pete, hold this for a minute, I have to make a phone call. I'll be right back."

"Is that your new girlfriend?" Molly asked.

"Not so new," Peter said. "We've been together for a while now."

"Since before the fire?"

"Yep," he said, after thinking back for a minute.

When Daisy had started dying, Trudy became more and more belligerent, finally getting beaten by a cop with his nightstick at a demonstration at Macy's and then getting kicked in the back a few months later at the Stock Exchange. Around the time of her second beating, her sister Sam got off drugs for two months and later for two weeks.

"Are you kidding me?" Molly said. "You mean all this time that Kate and I were running around protecting your ego you had another girlfriend?"

"Well, you've got to take care of your own needs," Peter said.

"Thanks for the advice."

After his death the bulk of Horne's holdings had been purchased by the president of a major chemical company who was himself assassinated by a man dying of cancer.

"Well, I gotta go," Molly said sliding off her counter stool.

"To a demonstration?" he asked, smiling.

"As a matter of fact, yes. I'm going to Saint Vincent's Hospital, where a man dying of AIDS was called 'fucking faggot' by a security guard in the emergency room."

"Well, good luck," he said. "You approach the world your way and I'll approach it mine. 'Let a thousand flowers bloom,' said Mao Tse-tung, right?"

Molly went into the cold toward James's house. She had been rather soft-spoken lately. She was conserving her energy. She didn't hang out much and liked to read *People* magazine, listen to the radio and sleep in her clothes. It was a saturation therapy. On the way to his apartment, she was thinking about how sometimes the city gets so beautiful that it's impossible to walk even one block without getting an idea. The idea she got was to try to remember the truth and not just the stories.

The others were waiting for her in James's living room where they had been trying to come up with a plan for a demo at the Meadowlands for the next Jets game.

"We only have an hour before we have to meet the others at Saint Vincent's," James said. "So let's try to get this meeting over with quickly. Here is a map of the stadium." He handed out Xeroxed sketches. "Now, the goal of this action is to give women support for asking men to wear condoms, right?"

"Right," said Jo-Jo, a recently recruited gay skinhead who came to Justice on his skateboard, even in the snow.

"So, we've made up these bumper stickers to put on all the cars in the parking lot. They say 'Men, Use Condoms or Beat It.' Jo-Jo, what's your report?"

"Well," he said, putting his jackboots up on the coffee table. "I called up Trojan, like you said, and they will donate ten thousand free condoms for us to distribute to men and women as they go into the stadium."

Molly sat back into the cushions on the couch. She was very tired. She held a warm cup of tea in her hands and brought it to her face. The radiators knocked. The winds rattled the shaky windowpanes.

"I'm tired," she said.

"I'm tired too," James said.

"So many people are so self-satisfied," Molly said. "They sit around, they don't do anything."

"Suffering can be stopped," James said. "But it can never be avenged, so survivors watch television. Men die, their lovers wait to get sick. People eat garbage or worry about their careers. Some lives are more important than others. Some deaths are shocking, some invisible. We are a people in trouble. We do not act."

Then everyone went to Saint Vincent's because there was nothing more to say.